Elusive

BRIAN SANDERS

Published by Underground Media

www.undergroundglobal.org

© 2010 Underground Media

Cover Design by Dan Niver
Interior Design by Angela Self

For information or bulk orders:
UNDERGROUND MEDIA
1300 E 7TH AVE
TAMPA, FL 33605
813.248.3301

Library of Congress Cataloging in Publication Data is available upon request.

ISBN 978-0-9845758-0-0

Printed in the United States of America

undergroundmedia

To Luke Judah

for teaching us all the humility of laughter

introduction

Who am I to write a book? Any book really. It takes a certain amount of confidence to think that people could or should benefit from your thoughts written down. Is it pride? It is hard for me not to think so. My approach is twofold. First, I just write. I try not to think about people reading it or not. There has to be some inner struggle or journey that is worth taking even if no one will ever know. Then I wrestle with whether or not it should be printed for others. Sometimes, it shouldn't. That is a hard enough distinction to make. But a book on humility? Come on. That is just too much. I wrote this manuscript in 1998. At the time, I could not find anything in mainstream Christian publishing on the subject. I had to go all the way back to Andrew Murray's 19th century classic to enter the conversation on what I thought was the seminal virtue of our time. I sent the manuscript to a publisher. There response was cold. The actual rejection letter said, "People are not interested in reading a book on humility, maybe a chapter, but not an entire book." I was stunned. Not that this little book was not worthy to be published, but that a lack of interest was the reason. People don't want to read a whole book on humility? I understand. If a book won't sell, why waste the time, money and resources to publish it. But there was such a void. I just thought the virtue, more than any other in our time, needed reflection and application.

The manuscript sat unread for over a decade. A decade that saw no less than a dozen books published in the mainstream on the subject of humility. Excellent writers and leaders are again interested in the revolutionary quality of the chief of all virtues, and not only are they writing, but apparently people are reading. I do feel a little vindicated. And it just did not seem right for this little manuscript to stay obscured on my back up hard drive. I want it to see the light of day, albeit a little late, I want to rejoin the public conversation about what I still consider the most difficult and important struggle of my life, the battle for humility.

Brian Sanders
December 2009

original
introduction

I realize that for those who know me the topic and author combination is thick with irony. The conceptual pursuit of humility, for me, is born out of a deeper yearning to see it practically in my life. It is precisely because I struggle that I have pursued the subject. My obvious failures are what make humility so important to me and so necessary for my own pilgrimage away from sin and toward God.

The people I most admire are humble. I am drawn to this elusive virtue when I see it in others, and it is what most captivates me about the life of Jesus. That is not to say that I do not recognize in Jesus other virtues, I do, but I am so unfamiliar with the consistent, courageous exercise of this virtue that when I see Jesus I am undone. I long to be like Christ, to imitate God—to let Christ live in me. I know that I can not do that without humility. Therefore, what I most lack I most crave. This book then is not for those who understand and exercise humility. It is not written by someone who is passing on their expertise or experience on the subject. This book is for all those who long for humility because we are painfully aware of our lack. It is for anyone who wants to be like Jesus in every way, even in attitude, and realize they are not. All I offer here are my thoughts as a seeker of this virtue, and the life of Christ, in the greater context of pursuing God. The more I have thought about, read about, and prayed for humility the more profoundly I have realized not only my own need but the churches need to present Jesus in the way he presented himself, in humility. My conclusion is that effective, authentic Christianity and the ministry that flows out of it can only be done in humility. Our lust for power in every form has lead to a loss of love for this virtue, which was intended to characterize everything we do, including great feats of power. Just as I was rescued and revolutionized by the humble act of God, so the world will only be changed by a message whose meaning is conveyed in this kind of radical language.

Brian Sanders
May 1998

contents

Part 4: Self

Part 5: Others

Part 6: Pride

Part 7: Love

humility

*All this tends to confirm that humility is
one of the chief and highest graces.
It is one of the most difficult to attain,
and one to which our first and greatest
efforts ought to be directed.*
                                    -Andrew Murray

the elusive truth

A few years ago just after Hurricane Katrina rocked New Orleans, I was knocking plaster off a water damaged wall in the Lower Ninth Ward, trying to be helpful. Our ministry team was having some meetings in New Orleans so we split our time doing some rehab work on a house in need of repair. My left hand was in an old window sill, for balance. My right hand hammering plaster off the damaged wall. The window came down on my fingers, severing about an inch of my middle finger. I did not even bother to look at it. We just jumped into the car looking for a hospital.

On the way, one of my teammates called us. "Dude, we found your finger, do you want it?" I said yes. We went back for it. The doctor did the best he could to reattach it, but in the end I lost that part of my finger. A little piece of me I lost in New Orleans. For a few years I had trouble with things like typing, and I still have a dull pain at the end of that finger. But now I have mostly adjusted. I still can't play guitar, but I have moved on. I just forget what it is like to have that part of my finger.

Every once in a while I remember. The other day, I tried to pick up some screws with my left hand. I couldn't do it. You don't realize how useful that piece of your finger is until it is missing. I just pinched and pinched. But the thumb had nothing to push against and no matter how hard I tried I could not pick up those screws. It was frustrating.

For most of my life as a Christian, I have wanted to be humble. The people that I most admire do it naturally. I, on the other hand, bumble on toward a virtue that only seems to become more and more elusive. Grabbing and pinching for something that is just not there. It's not like I am not trying, it is that trying doesn't actually help. It's like I have lost something, a part of my soul that is required for grasping humility. There is nothing for the thumb to press against. I reach for humility, and it just slips through my inadequate fingers.

Something somewhere happened to me, to us, that has made us proud. The misunderstanding is that this condition is a deformity, a handicap in our hearts. But we forget. We think we are whole. We think we are capable. We are proud. We may want very much to add humility to our battery of virtues, but it is not something capable people add to their repertoire. When we do that, it just slips away. For me it is the most elusive virtue.

Somewhere deep beneath the roots of humility is surrender, the kind that is self- sufficient, overly educated people always seem to struggle with. It requires an honest admission that I am flawed, not just in some things, but in all things. I just struggle to do that, to really mean it. To compound my folly, I am ruthlessly impatient of the struggle in others. Humility's absence in others stands like a monument of my own lack, as I find myself overly critical and intolerant of pride in everyone. This disdain only adds to the evidence of my own malady. C.S. Lewis said of the lack of humility in others, "There is no fault which makes a man more unpopular, and no fault which we are more unconscious of in ourselves. And the more we have it in ourselves the more we dislike it in others."[2] I say with ongoing sadness, that in others I abhor pride and adore humility, yet in myself I coddle my pride and am suspicious of humility.

To me humility is powerful. It is the restraint of greatness. I am so drawn to it and it is perhaps the quality that most impresses me about Jesus and most mystifies me about the Christian life. Just below the surface of his epic, world shaking life, there is a kind of shyness that I find so incalculable. In every interaction with sinners and saints alike, think of all the things Jesus does not say. Knowing all he knew, being so qualitatively superior to everyone he met, how did he restrain himself so profoundly? I think of all the ignorance he must have endured, how did he not just constantly correct people? I know I would have. It was actually quite rare. Of course, he did correct people's misconceptions about his Father, but even then it was often done with a kind of grace I find hard to grasp when I know I am right. Most of this book is really just my own journey after humility; a search for that shyness in my competence and confidence in my weakness. I am, slowly and after many years of struggle, learning to see the beauty and power in self-restraint, and embracing it in my own life.

The biblical mandate to "humble yourself"[3] has haunted me as I have too often preferred to take a passive approach to the subject, holding out for some alternative to this direct and personal command. The biblical impression that we are co-laborers with God in the business of sanctification is mind boggling, but it seems clear that a condition must exist before God exalts me: I must humble myself. How much energy do we really expend toward that end? It is a biblical command. It is a command that comes with a promise of blessing and grace. Still, we seem to have very little interest in it.

God is just and he is the great equalizer. While the goal of sanctification is to be presented pure to Jesus as his bride, the Holy Spirit provides what is lacking in this process toward righteousness. God is not capricious, he is fair. If we exalt ourselves he will bring us low. If we humble ourselves, then he will exalt. The time and place is undetermined, but this troubling promise applies to us all. What is most vexing to me, has been learning not to let exaltation be the goal, to pursue humility as a means to an end, namely greatness. This may be missing the point.

I have always wanted to achieve things. Now that I am a Christian, I still have that desire to do things for God. Like a child, I am communicating to God that I would like for him to cover his eyes, while I produce a surprise for him; a life well lived, ministry done, passionate worship, sincere prayer, etc. This desire to want to surprise God is not only impossible, but it is also offensive to his sovereignty. In a subtle way I am trusting my own ability, declaring my independence and investing the little faith I have into my own creative work.

In spite of my delusion, God does not close his eyes, and he is pleased with my gift only to the degree that I have let him create through me. He is always working in me, "For who makes you different from anyone else? What do you have that you did not receive? And if you did receive it, why do you boast as though you did not?"[4] The boast is the illusion of pride.

I have discovered the path toward humility is tread over my misconceptions about God and me. Pride lives in the lies we tell ourselves. Humility requires, at first, a change of heart and a new way of thinking. That is, in part, why I am writing these thoughts down. It simply takes more than one hearing to undo what decades of life and experience have taught us. Rest assured you and I are not sufficient. Contrary to popular teaching, you are not the maker of your own destiny and the giant inside you, if awakened, may lead to financial and worldly success, but it will devour your spiritual life in the process. C.S. Lewis wrote, "Pride leads to every other vice; it is the complete anti-God state of mind."[5]

chapter 2

the divine paradigm

One theme I want to explore in the chapters ahead is the idea of Jesus' life as a model for us. Friedrich Nietzsche, considered one of the most original thinkers of the 20th century, has influenced us more profoundly than we know. His philosophy embodied this human malady and revealed the deepest darkness of the human heart. In an attempt to establish the human strength above all else, he knew that the heart always reaches for something greater. Like, we want to believe we are great, but in our more lucid moments, we see who we really are and long for some deity that must be better. Nietzsche knew he would have to deal with the God problem in order to establish human supremacy. He chose murder. What greater demonstration of physical power over another is there? When he declared that God was dead and that we had killed him, we had deified "nothingness, the will to nothingness and pronounced it Holy."[6]

The Phoenix that would arise from the ashes of the God we killed would be the superman. Nietzsche contended that human beings were all that was left from the rubble of God's destruction and the world was in our hands to build or to destroy.[7] The only precursor to power is the human will.

By and large, the life of the western Christian is one of what has been called practical atheism. We are more like Nietzsche than we care to admit. We say we believe in God, but then we do not live lives conformed to his image. We live self-sufficient, self-concerned, and most importantly, self-governed lives, as if God were not God. We live as if he were not there. No matter what we say, pride betrays our atheism. There is such a thing as the Christian superman. We kill the image of God with our self-indulgence. It is all painfully cruciform.

I believe that Jesus would respond to our Nietzschian hubris in two ways. As for humanity, we are utter failures, feeble, petty, corrupt and collectively dangerous. If you give us something beautiful, give us enough time, we will corrupt and eventually destroy it. The fact that we are, on occasion, capable of love and kindness only makes our consistent neglect of that capacity an even greater scandal. I don't know much about insanity as a legal defense for a crime, (only what I have learned from watching Law and Order), but it seems like the way to make that case is to demonstrate that the accused had no ability to determine right from wrong. In other words, I am not responsible for something when I cannot distinguish right from wrong. Our ability to do good and then choose not to, proves that we are not insane, just wicked (and proud of it). While proud and assured, our confidence is unfounded and our arrogance the bastion of our deepest corruption. Upon honest reflection, we know there is nothing super about man.

As for God, he is of course not dead, not to say we did not kill him--we did. But he arose, says the gospel writers, and that is good news indeed, because his death meant the end of sin, if we would have it. Our hero was the only real life superman. For God himself became man to show us how it was done. We have made a mockery of a divine image and Jesus came, in part, to show us what a real human life was to look like. So, for the Christian, the life of Christ is the beginning and the end of our search for meaning and significance. This is where we look for how to live. His life is the divine paradigm, not only for what we do, but how we do it.

While this is one thing to say, it is quite another to really live. First, we do not fully perceive his life. We tend to be selective in the portrait we paint of this God-life. Some of us emphasize forgiveness but not judgment, love but not justice, truth without mercy, or tolerance lacking passion. We explain the life of Christ in terms we find palatable or fashionable, with little regard to the revolutionary nature of the incarnation.

Second, we know we can not live it fully so we do not try. We buckle under the pressure of our world and admire the life of Jesus from afar, relegating it to a bygone era of robes and sandals, uncomplicated by the complexity of modern life.

Lastly, we don't realize that we should be like Jesus. We see Jesus as our savior but not our Lord. We graciously thank him for the work of the cross, doing away with our sin, and the resurrection breaking the power of death over us. But we ignore his life and teaching. In the words of James Stewart, "Christianity does not mean complementing Christ as genius, or artist, or teacher: it means bowing to Christ as commander."[8]

God knew that we learn best by illustration. Conceivably, God could have suffered and even died without our knowledge. He could have atoned for sin privately. But he lived and died for all to see, illustrating the perfect life, the life we are to imitate. For those of us who are however, convinced that the life of Jesus is not simply incidental, there are considerable challenges still to overcome.

In my estimation, there is no more difficult aspect of his great life to imitate than his humility. It means the utter rejection of our own pride (which is difficult enough) and then the embrace of the most profound expression of love possible.

moving toward humility

Moving toward the model of Jesus starts with the acknowledgement that we are not like him. The first step to humility is to realize that we lack it. It is to recognize and admit, "I am proud." It is of course not that simple. It is like the old joke, "I won a medal for being humble, but I wore it so they took it away." If we claim to be humble, then we are by necessity not. "If you think you are not conceited, it means you are very conceited indeed."[9] The problem with this cycle is that people will vehemently admit they are prideful, not because they see the evil behind their attitude, but because they know that if they do not admit it they will not be considered humble. This admission then is false. Simply because someone says, "I could be wrong," but has never to anyone's knowledge, including himself, been wrong on a specific occasion, it is doubtful whether he truly means he could be wrong. I have been in confessional situations where someone admits to struggling with pride. Curiously, it is not actually a humble act. Not all such confessions are disingenuous but some can be almost counter intuitive. As if they are saying, "Please pray for me, I am struggling with pride. You see I am convinced I am better than everyone. That's my great struggle. In the face of such giftedness and accomplishment, I am really having trouble believing that I am not superior to everyone." I scratch my head thinking, "Dudes are confessing real dirty stuff, humbling themselves to do it, and this guy is saying he struggles with pride?" It just doesn't fit. Not that pride is not dirty; it may be the dirtiest sin of all. But it is possible to be proud of our pride.

Pride must be starved. It can not be given any daylight to announce itself. Humility expressed in contrition is its antidote. If you struggle with pride, the Bible is clear what to do. Humble yourself. Confess something that would embarrass you, not make you seem awesome. Confronting pride in ourselves is a gruesome task. It is quite uncomfortable and will produce nothing less than a loathing for its remaining remnant.

chapter 4

imitation

The progression toward humility begins with the realization of the divine paradigm, the lengths we go to reject it, and a conscious turning toward it and its practice. Just trying to be humble is hard though, maybe impossible, certainly unnatural. The secret is worship. The life of humility and the life of worship are the same. And worship is the more accessible practice.

Humility is not only the necessary posture toward God in worship, but it is, itself, the most profound act of worship. There is no greater compliment we can pay to God above imitation. The re-enactment of the life of Jesus, in every detail, is the living song of respect and veneration to the servant King. That means not only reliving the external life of sacrifice and self-denial but also the hidden, perhaps more unique, inner life of abasement and preference for others. What is most incredible about the sacrifice of the cross is not that a man would willingly give his life for a cause, or even a person, but that Jesus, in the fullness of deity, knew that his life was to be a ransom for those who despised him. The motive is what has not and will not be matched in all of human history.

Humility was the inward reality of the character of Christ, expressed in outward acts of sacrifice and self-denial. Human beings have never had a problem imitating sacrifice. The challenge, of course, is to not exalt in the experience. False humility longs to be seen. Once we recognize the wonder and glory of the humility of Jesus, we can label it a virtue, a characteristic to be achieved and added to one's repertoire. It then becomes yet another potential source of pride for us. As such a source it not only undermines the process of attaining it, but also destroys what little humility we might have. This is what makes humility so elusive.

Like spiritual greatness, it can not be attained by a direct campaign. If I try to be humble, I am not. "I would not advise any of you to try to be humble," Charles Spurgeon preached. "As to acting humbly, when a man forces himself to it, that is poor stuff. When a man talks a great deal about his humility, when he is very humble to everybody, he is generally a canting hypocrite."[10] If I try to be great in the Kingdom, if that is my goal, then I will never be more than a second rate actor trying to imitate Jesus, who gave up greatness for service, whose life was worship to God and love for others.

Ironically, Jesus himself was never as intolerant of a sin as he was of this one. The Pharisees boasted in their religious life. They took pride in themselves not for things they did not do, but for their actual accomplishments. Nothing was so deeply offensive to Jesus (and his Father) and nothing elicited such a merciless response from Jesus. As G.K. Chesterton puts it, "The man who is proud of what is really credible to him is the Pharisee, the man whom Christ Himself could not forbear to strike."[11] Mohammed Ali once touted, "If you can do it, it ain't braggin." But, whether or not one is actually capable does not make the sin of boasting less reprehensible. Jesus refused to overlook it. There was not a deeper malady to confront. When pride lifted up its boast before Jesus he could not and would not remain silent.

This is significant because Jesus was often silent in the presence of sin. Certainly, Jesus was always teaching and encouraging those who had ears toward the Kingdom of his Father, but when in the presence of what might today be considered some of the most egregious sins, Jesus spoke of other things.

When I think of all the errors that today's Christians can not tolerate, I wonder if we have the mind of Christ at all. Like us today, there were things that Jesus simply could not sit idly by and let happen around him without an outraged cry of righteous indignation. We too should take a stand on things that must be confronted. But let us look to Jesus to determine what those things are. For Jesus it was not things like drinking, or prostitution, or homosexuality. Certainly, Jesus did not condone these behaviors, but in their presence he did not choose to scold sinners but to deliver good news about the kingdom of God.

Likewise, he did not seem interested in the considerable political injustice of the day. The spurious Roman occupation was not holy yet; it was not the issue Jesus chose to become indignant over. The sin he could not stand was hypocrisy.

chaper 5

the inner life

The word hypocrisy comes from the character Hypocrites, who is regarded as the first Greek thespian. Literally, "one who wears a mask." The implications are obvious. An actor is by definition two-faced, they "play" a role, and they get into a character that is not at all who they are. Jesus accused the Pharisees of being actors in a great religious drama, two-faced fakers who might fool others but who would not escape the penetrating gaze of God.

> Everything they do is done for men to see: They make their phylacteries wide and the tassels on their garments long; they love the place of honor at banquets and the most important seats in the synagogues; they love to be greeted in the marketplaces and to have men call them 'Rabbi.' But you are not to be called 'Rabbi,' for you have only one Master and you are all brothers.

> And do not call anyone on earth 'father,' for you have one Father, and he is in heaven. Nor are you to be called 'teacher,' for you have one Teacher, the Christ. The greatest among you will be your servant. For whoever exalts himself will be humbled, and whoever humbles himself will be exalted.[12]

They saw their lives as being lived on a stage before people. The goal was to put on a good act and to be believable, so the crowd would go away thinking they were someone they were not.

I cannot help but draw a comparison to the contemporary mega church. I do not want to disparage any church form; especially one that, in many cases, has born tremendous fruit for the kingdom. But we have to be honest about the shadows these massive churches cast. Regardless of their relative strengths and weaknesses, missiologically, leaders in these churches face formidable temptations being on stage. This form could be characterized, church as spectacle. And there is no one more in the spotlight than the leaders. Like Pharisees they face the challenge of living a life in the public eye.

My own heart is imperiled every time I step onto a platform to preach or lead. The dangerous and insidious combination of our North American celebrity culture, along with our innate pride, intermingles to damage the souls of our leaders. In some cases even destroy them. Where is the shyness of Jesus in our leaders, as they telecast themselves into satellite services around the city or even the world? This kind of breakdown in humility should shock and concern us, but it does not because we have conspired with our leaders to prefer their false self to the real one.

If we love our leaders, we will not follow them in their pride, nor place them under the spotlight of Christian spectacle. And all of us stand warned. Humility cannot survive the scrutiny of stage lights. Humility has to be cultivated in private. It will not thrive on stage.

Life offers a series of pitfalls in this area. For the Pharisees, and potentially for the disciples, religious titles were such a pitfall. Certainly, the titles Rabbi and Father are not intrinsically wrong, Jesus himself was called Rabbi. Yet, the title had become a badge worn by the proud and what was supposed to be a position of service and responsibility had become a source of personal pride and was forthrightly prohibited by Jesus. Titles usually are only good for vertical distinctions. Superiority is almost always implied in them. Even a lowly title, "town drunk" or "garbage man" implies expertise or superiority in some area, even if it is undesirable. In the end titles delineate. That is the point. We just don't need them. Jesus gives his friends this injunction because titles historically don't help the soul to achieve humility. His advice was to consider Jesus the only Master and Teacher, and God the only Father, so that God would be exalted and they would be brothers.

Jesus taught that life comes from death. "I tell you the truth, unless a kernel of wheat falls to the ground and dies, it remains only a single seed. But if it dies, it produces many seeds."[13] Like a seed that dies and then comes to life underground, so the human heart must be rightly aligned to God out of sight. Then, and only then, can we begin to grow out of our private lives into a public expression of an inward reality of humility toward God and others.

chapter 6

inside
the cup

As children, every Easter morning my sister and I would rush out of our rooms to inspect our Easter baskets. They would have other candies but the real centerpiece, the point really, was the chocolate bunny. The plastic grass, the basket, the rest of the candy was really just the stage for the bunny. I still remember the first time I realized that bunny was hollow. Biting into the ear and then looking down into the hollow body was a bona fide childhood tragedy. When I go to the store today around Easter time, I find that those bunnies are rarely solid anymore. It has become understood that unless indicated on the package, the bunny, whatever size it appears to be, is hollow. People know that Easter bunnies are hollow. They accept it. To be solid is an exception.

Years later a friend of mine reminded me of that experience, and he likened it to the disappointment he has had in the unveiling of the contemporary Christian. I fear that he is right. That it is the exception today to find a Christian that is sincere, solid on the inside. So much of what we esteem in the church is an external, physical spirituality. We have made it more important to be able to excel at praying out loud than praying in private (against the strict injunction of Jesus in Matthew 6.) We are hardest on external sins like addiction and sexual immorality which bring shame, and we neglect the deeper internal sins like greed and pride, which destroy us from the inside out. We have acquiesced to a kind of moral and spiritual capitalism that invests in what will bring the greatest immediate returns. Like the Pharisees, who undoubtedly began with a sincere desire to know and follow God, we have preferred the wide fast road of self-esteem instead of the narrow, slow road of self-denial that comes from humility.

For more than a decade I worked with college students, and it always amazed me at how quickly a person who comes to Christ is transformed externally. Within a year, a new believer will know all the relevant and frequently quoted Bible verses of a fellowship (although they may not know where they are). They will have learned to avoid all the unpardonable sins of a group. They will have learned the appropriate nomenclature, and within a matter of months no one can tell how long they have been a Christian. I do not mean to minimize the sanctifying work of the Holy Spirit in the life of a new believer, but I do mean to question the standard of Christian maturity. Shouldn't those who have walked with Jesus the longest most reflect his likeness?

Whatever we esteem as essential to the Christian life, new believers will invest in. Unfortunately, what I see is that we stress the necessity of a transformation in the external life, which is measurable and obvious, and not the internal life, which is more critical. "The Lord does not look at the things man looks at. Man looks at the outward appearance, but the Lord looks at the heart."[14] Paul reiterated "God does not judge by external appearance."[15] Or as Tertullian put it, "Do the ears of God wait for sound?"[16]

Humility will continue to elude me if I do not begin to deliberately invest in my inner life. Too much energy is expended to maintain the exterior, which only produces a false sense of spiritual success. If that means my external life suffers, so be it. Of course, I do not think the journey inward will have negative consequences for the outward life. Jesus taught that good trees bear good fruit. They do not have to strain to produce what is the fruit of their identity. When investment is made for the building of the inner person, the result is a righteous life, and a genuine one at that. Spurgeon argued that "humility must be in the heart, and then it will come out spontaneously as the outflow of life in the very act that a man performs."[17]

Humility eludes us because we can not embrace it as long as we simultaneously embrace our pride. We must rid ourselves of any vestige of our own righteousness and desire only God. John Calvin wrote, "Christian humility consists in laying aside the imaginary idea of our own righteousness, and trusting entirely to the mercies of God, apprehended by faith in Christ."[18] In the throws of neediness is where greatness is found. To whatever degree we proclaim our sufficiency we also proclaim his insufficiency. Even in the pursuit of this virtue it can never eclipse the pursuit of God. The secret to embracing humility is embracing the life of Jesus, as it really is. To follow him is to carry a cross not to wear a crown. That is for later.

When I saw him, I fell at his feet as though dead.
                                    -Revelation 1:17

chapter 7

humility begins with awe

I sat in silence in the balcony of the church with my best man sitting next to me. I didn't say anything; what was there to say at that moment? I looked down upon the assembling crowd and my stomach knotted. Maybe it was the fact that I had consumed two, possibly three six packs of Yoo-Hoo the night before (it's hard to explain), or the fact that all I had eaten in two days was a couple of buttermilk biscuits with sausage gravy, I don't know. Even the biscuits seemed to be threatening revolt at that moment.

I remember feeling alone. There was a place in the front of that sanctuary where only I could stand and a great responsibility that only I could fulfill. I was the only person that seemed to exist—that seemed to matter, at that moment. We made some jokes; I tried to act like I was not nervous. I eventually took my place.

As the wedding march began to play I went numb, and it was at the sight of my bride that my nervousness vanished. For a split second no one existed on earth but her. I was not nervous because I was no longer aware of myself. Her brightness, her glory demanded attention and her beauty consumed me. She was the centerpiece; all eyes were on her, and all my thoughts, wondering about hers. It was not necessarily something that I reasoned in my mind to do. I did not concentrate on her so I could get my mind off myself (which is still self-centered). I was a captive to her glory; I was in awe. This is the starting place for the humble.

Awe is a kind of self-forgetting. It is perfect awareness of another. For one moment in time, how I felt, what I thought, even my identity was irrelevant. Humility begins with awe. So that is where we must also begin.

It seems to me the church of Jesus Christ is crippled where it has thought that the Christian life, the Christ-life, can be lived without humility. Somehow it has been buried behind other values prescribed in our unique North American cultural identity. Subjugated behind independence, intelligence, charisma and others, humility is not really necessary to being perceived as a "successful" Christian in our society, in our time. While sages extol humility as one of the chief virtues, if not the primary virtue, we treat it as optional. Yet, there was nothing Jesus did that was not colored with this difficult and enigmatic virtue. It is hard to reward, it can not be achieved in the formal sense, and it is often lost as it is directly pursued. Humility can not stand the stage and therefore can not be codified the way generosity or even love can be. In other words, it is not gained by a direct campaign but is somehow a product of something else. This book in large part is about that "something else." It is about imitating the life of Christ, that was, in my opinion, quintessentially humble.

In order to develop lives that are more similar to the life that Jesus meant for us, we have somehow to embody this virtue. Just as in the life of Jesus, every aspect of the Christian life (evangelism, community, discipleship, and worship), all have to be characterized by humility. I believe this journey begins at the same place it ends, in the awe that comes from an encounter with the glory of God.

The late German sociologist of religion Rudaulph Otto, in his study on the origin of religion, concluded that all religions find their genesis in awe, what he calls *mysterium tremendom*.[19] Otto catalogs the common human experience of wonder that impresses a person with a deep and profound sense of God. According to Otto, it often occurs in a confrontation with nature. If you have ever stood at the summit of a mountain or the edge of the Grand Canyon, or looked out on the endless ocean horizon, then you may be able to relate. Otto's conclusion is that all religion begins with a sense of awe.

He refers to an experience that explodes our sensual categories, and if only for a moment, fills us with both the knowledge of the existence of the infinite and a sense of our own insignificance. Otto could have saved some time by reading Romans 1. "Since what may be known about God is plain to them, because God has made it plain to them. For since the creation of the world God's invisible qualities--his eternal power and divine nature--have been clearly seen, being understood from what has been made, so that men are without excuse."[20] C.S. Lewis, in response to Otto, concluded there could only be two views concerning awe.

> Either it is a mere twist in the human mind, corresponding to nothing objective and serving no biological function, yet showing no tendency to disappear from that mind at its fullest development in poet, philosopher, or saint: or else it is a direct experience of the really supernatural, to which the name revelation might properly been given.[21]

According to Paul, the proper response to this kind of revelation is to glorify God and give him thanks.[22]

chapter **8**

theophany

There are plenty of memorable encounters between the infinite God and the finite creation in the Bible. The result is always awe. Job knew that God was awesome, and for him the realization of the awe and dread of a holy God was far greater in his suffering. He wrote these powerfully lucid words.

> Death is naked before God; Destruction lies uncovered. He spreads out the northern over empty space; he suspends the earth over nothing. He wraps up the waters in his clouds, yet the clouds do not burst under their weight. He covers the face of the full moon, spreading his clouds over it. He marks out the horizon on the face of the waters for a boundary between light and darkness. The pillars of the heavens quake, aghast at his rebuke. By his power he churned up the sea; by his wisdom

he cut Rahab to pieces. By his breath the skies became fair; his hand pierced the gliding serpent. *And these are but the outer fringe of his works; how faint the whisper we hear of him! Who then can understand the thunder of his power?"*[23] (Italics mine)

Job was a wise man. Even in his struggle with God he knew who God was and who he was. Wisdom follows awe, and humility comes from true wisdom. First we experience awe, then we develop wisdom that comes from tasting pure truth, and then humility is born out of that wisdom. "Who is wise and understanding among you? Let him show it by his good life, by deeds done in the *humility that comes from wisdom.*"[24] One glimpse into the greatness of God leaves the viewer naked before him. Pride is the ultimate lie. It is the great deception of the enemy to lure us into self-elevation and self-aggrandizement. Humility on the other hand is the product of worship, and worship is the experience and embrace of the truest reality. Worship reveals the truth; the truth about God in his infinite majesty, grace and terror, and the truth about us, in our fragile, broken, and wicked condition. This is the backdrop upon which God can display his mercy.

What happens in the presence of God? First, there is the realization of our sinfulness. Once we have had an audience with a holy God we can no longer continue the charade; "I am not so bad." When Isaiah experienced the theophany, he was undone. Isaiah sees the Lord for who He really is.[25] Isaiah sees the King of kings, "seated on the throne". He sees him "high and exalted", which is the only perspective from which to view God, an upward gaze. His initial reaction to pure perfection is to identify not only the imperfection in himself but also in his race, in human beings. "'Woe to me!' I cried. 'I am ruined! For I am a man of unclean lips, and I live among a people of unclean lips, and my eyes have seen the King, the LORD Almighty.'"[26]

We can not look at sin as a subtle nuisance, tainting our subdued greatness. Rather sin must become known for what it is, the mortal enemy of our souls seeking to devour us from the inside out. Even if preachers stop preaching about this insipid, cancerous disease, it has not changed. It is a disease, of which we all suffer, which has rendered us all invalids in need of a total healing. This truth actually empowers us to true and spiritual worship because it is only in utter dependence that God is rightly worshipped. When we are ultimately helpless he is ultimate to us. We see our sin that contributes to our humbling, but it is not the primary catalyst, the greatness of God is. In order for humility to characterize us as people, God must first be magnified. God has to be regarded differently, as greater. We need a theophany.

When Job saw the Lord out of the storm he was left with one conclusion, "My ears had heard of you but now my eyes have seen you. Therefore I despise myself and repent in dust and ashes."[27]

When Peter met Jesus his first response was pride in his own knowledge of his trade. However, once he recognized the power of God in Jesus he was left groveling, "Go away from me, Lord; for I am a sinful man."[28]

All of the disciples saw the resurrected Jesus and they "clasped his feet, and worshipped him."[29] Likewise, when John saw the glorified Jesus, "he fell at his feet as though dead."[30]

Ezekiel didn't see God, or his glory, or the likeness of it. Rather, he saw only the appearance of the likeness of the glory of YAHWEH, and he could not keep his feet.[31] Awe leads to humility.

The experience of divine light not only exposes darkness, but it also purifies. God does not leave us in our ruin. Once Isaiah experienced the awe of the presence of God, he knew the truth about himself and his people and the truth about the greatness of God. He repented and God forgave. "With it he touched my mouth and said, 'See, this has touched your lips; your guilt is taken away and your sin atoned for.'" [32] That, however, is not the end of the theophany.

God does not employ humility solely for the purpose of humiliating us. He knows that unless we have a change of perspective, a change of heart, and unless we embrace reality we can not live life the way he intended it. His ultimate concern for us is restoration.

So, Isaiah, repentant and forgiven, was then sent to be a vessel of God.[33] Job was made twice as prosperous as he was before.[34] Peter was commissioned to become a fisher of men, and the rock of Christ's church.[35] The disciples rose to receive the Great Commission.[36] John received the touch of the glorified God who says, "Do not be afraid", and was instructed to write all that he would see.[37] Ezekiel would have probably liked to have remained face down, but God's voice always says to the humble, "Stand up on your feet, and I will speak to you."[38]

"But if you harbor bitter envy and selfish ambition in your hearts, do not boast about it or deny the truth. Such 'wisdom' does not come down from heaven but is earthly, unspiritual, of the devil."[39] To exalt ourselves is to deny the truth, to deny reality—of which God is the center. The counterfeit wisdom of pride elevates me, if only a little, beyond my actual position, so that I might think more of myself than I ought. This alternative wisdom, according to James is from the devil, who is himself a victim of skewed reality.[40]

chapter 9

the divine
center

If we lack humility it is because we first lack the awe that comes from a divine center. Most of us attempt to understand ourselves relative to those around us. This is a grave error. We set ourselves at the center of our world and then proceed to access the relative merit, and/or flaws of those around us. So, our conception of humility is not completely absent; it is simply impaired because it lacks a divine center. Our concept of humility is situational.

For instance, when I go out to play basketball I am very aware of those around me. Without much effort I can size up the competition and determine where I fit in the pecking order on that particular day. If I accidentally stumble into a gym where several NBA players happen to be looking for a pickup game, I quickly become "humble". That is, I say very little about my jump shot or ball handling skills, and if I speak at all it is an *act* of contrition or a plea for mercy. At the very least

I offer a disclaimer, "Hey guys, I am not very good so take it easy on me." In fact, given that situation I may be so "humbled" that I will not even consider myself worthy to play with them.

If, however, on the same day I show up and the players appear to be mediocre, flailing around, dribbling the ball off their feet and struggling to make a shot, then I approach very differently. My head is high, my chest inflated, I dribble the ball between my legs and confidently declare, "I got next." The question is: Am I a humble person or am I a prideful person? Who am I really? Most of us, if put into an intimidating enough situation, will act humbly. That is situational humility. It is nothing like the humility of Christ, which remained intact in spite of the situation. Christ who was superior to everyone he ever came in contact with (in every way that matters) rarely asserted himself. Humility for Jesus was just a given regardless of the context. The real challenge for us is not being humble when we are weak or wrong, but when we think we are strong or right.

The last few years has seen a renaissance in a concern for orthodox theology. The decade of the '90s saw so many people come to Christ experientially that there was often an absence of a theological or biblical foundation. It seemed like the '90s was about experiencing God and not reasoning our way toward him. That is of course a good thing. The down side has been those people who came to Christ in that generation are not as grounded theologically, and as they have become the leaders of the new church, planting, and establishing new and creative ministry expressions, there has (in my opinion) been a loss of proper theological perspective.

Some liberties have been taken by some of these "post modern" leaders that have troubled us. I understand that. This has solicited a reaction, especially from our reformed brothers and sisters. They have come out hard against some of these leaders, calling for biblical orthodoxy. The publishing of blogs and books have acted as a kind of dialogical corrective, and I am grateful for that. The problem is that this corrective has often been mean spirited, misinformed and even slanderous. Christian leaders are actually calling people out by name and dusting off words like heretic and apostate. It staggers me. I have even been the object of some of this critique, and I believe wrongfully so. But the end result is a "truth" that is untrue because it is not gracious, honor born, or humble.

In this case humility demands two realities: first, the acknowledgement that we are all heretics in ways we don't realize, and we should therefore be merciful in all things. Second, humility reveals most when we are right. Being humble when we are wrong is not near as important as when we are right. This was Jesus' great strength. One, we do not pursue as we should. Why not go and befriend these young, creative leaders with leaky theology? Why not be fathers and friends to them by challenging them out of loving relationship and first hand information? Many of these leaders have committed their whole lives to good news of the Kingdom of God and to the glory of Jesus. They are not perfect, and neither are you.

Humility is a condition of the heart that is unaltered by a change in context. Humility demands that the gaze of the heart be constantly fixed on the majesty of God. True humility has God as its center. As long as we are content to measure ourselves in human terms then we will always be better than someone. The illusion of our own righteousness will remain intact, only before God is it completely and utterly dismantled.

All of those who would call themselves Christian will have necessarily had to have experienced this truth, because salvation itself can not be imparted to us until we recognize our need. This neediness is not merely a one-time crisis of the soul. While the work of the cross is final, the business of sanctification is ongoing. At least a moment of true humility is necessary for salvation, but sanctification requires a lifetime of it.

Humility precedes grace because God has to be the source. As long as we contend for a role in our salvation (temporal or eternal), we will find ourselves defenseless. Charles Spurgeon made the point, "When you have found out what you really are, you will be humble for you are nothing to boast of."[41] Pride must be driven out by the light of the glory of God in the face of Christ Jesus.[42]

We lack humility because we deny the greatness of God, not so much in the open display of his power; even the devil is contrite then, but in the obscured revelation of his presence in the face of others. In ways that are hard to describe with words, God is with the weak, judging us there, in that place where he is strongest.

One of the more remarkable exhibitions of faith in the Bible is the thief who dies next to Jesus. Condemned on the same day as Jesus, two other men shared his fate of crucifixion. Luke describes the scene, Jesus, the creator of all things, hidden between criminals. One of them mocks him, "Aren't you the Christ? Save yourself and us!" The other one challenges them, "Don't you fear God?" "Jesus, remember me, when you come into your Kingdom." It's staggering. Who, at this point, believes that Jesus is the King of anything, or that he is about to come into the Kingdom? It is one of the purest most beautiful demonstrations of faith in Scripture. When all others see weakness and futility, this thief sees a King, and a Kingdom coming.

Jesus rewards this faith with the promise "you will be with me in paradise." But it calls to us the deepest of questions. Do we believe in God when he appears to be at his weakest? Not when nature is being bent to his will, bodies healed, or demons reviling in submission. When it appears that all is lost? Circumstance does not alter God; it only obscures the visage of his power.

Humility is saying that God is greater than we are. That our perception is limited, and that he has no peer, no counselor to question him. It is ridiculous to believe that our pride and his supremacy can coexist, they can not. John Calvin contended that humility is absent, "so long as we think there is any good remaining in us." With almost prophetic knowledge he further indicts, "Those who have joined together the two things, to think humbly of ourselves before God and yet hold our own righteousness in some estimation, have hitherto taught a pernicious hypocrisy."[43] As long as we retain a notion of our own righteousness, God is unknown. A return to the holy place of God will sanitize our wayward conceptions. The starting point for humility is awe in the presence of God.

chapter 10
neoinzing God

We have exchanged the manifold glory of God, which is only perceived by the eyes of the heart, for a Hollywood version of his greatness. Instead of his glory, we display his glamour; instead of his greatness, we advertise his usefulness. We build buildings and chisel, "to the glory of God" on the outside. But what about the building gives him glory? We spend exorbitant amounts of money on walls and windows all for the God who says "Don't you know that you yourselves are God's temple and that God's Spirit lives in you?"[44]

We take Bible verses that communicate the living Word of God and put them in fortune cookies or on mints. We package the faith, and trivialize God. We take the glory of God and compress it to fit into little neon tubes that we find beautiful, but in reality, they are gaudy, cheap expressions of the inexpressible greatness of God. Are not these vain attempts our own version of the Tower of Babel? Shouldn't we rather look to God himself for the mode through which he would be glorified? Our well-intentioned attempt to neonize him has only produced a counterfeit glory.

When God acts it is glorious. If we would glorify him we should imitate him. It is in the reenactment of the glorious deeds of God that he is most exalted and his truest splendor made manifest. God is not most glorified by great buildings or even great deeds. Rather, God is most glorified by the lowly acts of a contrite heart—that is, the imitation of a lowly savior, and the worship of a humble God.

chapter 11

the incarnational life of worship

The first verses of Ephesians 5 have captured my imagination. The verse begins, *"Be imitators of God, therefore, as dearly loved children."*[45]

The prescription for godliness is to imitate God. Paul gives the manor or character of that imitation, which is like the imitation of a child to her parent.

I have six children, ages 14 to 1. All of my kids have learned how to act from my wife and me. Much to my shame, even their flaws are little mirrors for us. What our kids see us do, they do. Children are not in a position to make value judgments about the appropriateness of a parent's behavior, or if it fits a personality profile, or even how it will "seem" to others, they simply imitate. This is the kind of imitation Paul is advocating. Simple enough, but the real mind bender is how are we supposed to imitate a God who is unseen?

John gives the answer. "The Word became flesh and made his dwelling among us,"[46] or as Jesus himself said, "If you have seen me you have seen the Father."[47] It is the call to incarnation, to let God become flesh again, in us. In the incarnation of Jesus, God became flesh so that in his body he could both do away with sin, and he could demonstrate the life we were meant to lead. When we imitate God, we allow that ideal life to be lived again in us. Paul continues,

"...and live a life of love, just as Christ loved us..."[48]

So as children who lovingly admire and reverence the life of a good parent, so we should faithfully live, "just as Christ" lived.

So then what does that look like? What is the essence of the imitation of Christ, of the incarnational life, the life of love?

"...and gave himself up for us as a fragrant offering and sacrifice to God."[49]

The image employed by Paul is one of temple worship, of an altar and of its fire and the smell of shed blood. The life of Christ was a life of worship and awe. Motivated by love, he laid his life upon the altar as a sacrifice for us. While it did serve the purpose of atonement it was also received as a fragrant or acceptable offering of worship to the Father. The sacrifice was for *us* but *to* God. So it is that the life we are to lead is a life of sacrifice for others which are at once, the imitation of Jesus and an act of worship to God. The life of humility is a life of worship because it reflects the life that perfectly glorified God, the life of Jesus.

The incarnational life is a life of worship. Often when we refer to worship the word conjures up images of singing, dancing, or liturgy. While these are viable expressions of a life of worship they are not the essential expression of worship. Here is how I am defining it: Worship is the total sacrifice of oneself to God. It is all of you for him, all of your hopes and fears, your career, your hobbies, all of your life a burnt offering on the altar of God.

Worship is the dedication of our selves to God in concert with creation. Worship is a celebration of the goodness of God and the embrace of reality. It is the proclamation of the Son of God and the remembrance of the cross. It is the rising of the glory of God through the light of his presence, it is the beloved loving of the redeemer, it is the declaration of the deeds of God, and it is a rehearsal of his unending mercy. *This is the essence of worship, to let Christ live through you.* Imitation then, is not only the highest form of flattery but it is also the highest form of worship. To imitate Jesus is to worship him.

There are three things that I see as hallmarks of this kind of life, three practical expressions of a life that imitates Jesus and is characterized by humility. A life of awe and worship is a life that is transformed by the gospel, a life that imitates Jesus, and a life that is given completely to God. This is the starting point for humility. Encountering God will mean a transformation of your old life, an imposition of a new life in its place, and daily surrender to that process.

chapter 12

a life
transformed
by the gospel

I find it interesting that in many parts of the world the church is experiencing revival and astonishing growth. The hub of Christianity is no longer in North America and Europe, but it is in places like Asia, and Africa, and Latin America. I recently read that in the forty years since the missionaries were forced to leave China, the evangelical population has exploded from an estimated 750,000 to 35 million, conservatively.[50] China and Brazil are now second and third respectively in the number of foreign missionaries sent overseas. (Some of which are being sent to the United States). In the last thirty years the population of evangelicals in Brazil alone has gone from 4 million to 26 million.[51] In Africa, at the turn of the century, there were an estimated 8.8 million Christians. Today there are 338 million.[52] In Uganda alone 80 percent of the population of 22 million, profess the name of Christ.[53]

Why is the church growing all over the world, while here it seems to be struggling? While I am not a sociologist and I do not propose to know entirely why, it seems that in these places, to be a Christian continues to carry a higher price. It can not be entered into lightly. Jesus is not simply the best option among many, the most convenient, or the most socially respectable. For many, becoming and remaining a Christian means the possibility of facing great suffering, alienation, and even death.

So why do they chose Jesus? It's because the gospel is real, and they have had a transforming encounter with it. News about a humble God, who would give himself for those he created, is revolutionary in countries where power rules and governments are validated by the size of their army and not their competence to govern. These Christians come in contact with the living God, a King who does not play by the rules of his wayward children, but comes as a baby in a stable to rule with love and sacrifice. They are different, because they have found Jesus to be reliable when he says, "whoever will lose his life for my sake will find it." They know what it means to give yourself to Christ, to lay your life on the altar, to give yourself as a fragrant offering to God.

My family and I live in the inner city of Tampa. We share our home with several students and people who are committed to the same vision on campus and in the inner city. Shortly after we had moved in we were up late, and having just said good-bye to some of our friends who were visiting, I began to get ready for bed.

At the time we had a student named Daniel living with us. He was also up late, studying for a test the next day, and in typical freshman form he was cramming. He informed me that he was going to need to be up for awhile and that he needed what all cramming college students need when such a night is before them: Mountain Dew. I offered to go with him, and I don't really know why but I suggested that we walk.

I knew there was a gas station a few blocks away and although it was after midnight it did not seem like such a big deal. I think I wanted to assert myself, as if to say, "This is my neighborhood too, and I can walk down the most dangerous street in Tampa at midnight if I want to." While there was not much humility there, there was a bit of faith and so we left.

I was shirtless, clad only in some old shorts and flip-flops, and Daniel was looking haggard from the last few hours of studying. The walk was about half a mile. Halfway there we began to get a little nervous. I became conscious of how I looked and every turn seemed ominous. We passed by a couple of prostitutes and smiled, not wanting to seem cold but not wanting to seem to friendly either, for obvious reasons. There were people lining the main strip which was the most direct route to the gas station but also the most conspicuous. I began to reevaluate my desire to stake a claim to the neighborhood. This was situational humility at its finest. But we walked on, knowing in a deeper place than our heads that we were under the divine protection of God.

Just then we were accosted. A man who had yelled something unintelligible to us moments before began running towards us. He approached us and stopped to ask one question.

"Y'all from around here?" Suspicion characterized his gaze, and somehow we knew the answer to this question was important.

"Yes, we are," I said, and I proceeded to point and describe where our house was. His demeanor changed and it became obvious to him that we were not up to any nefarious business and that although we appeared to be outsiders we were not.

"Oh. Well I have never seen you around before." he confessed. He seemed a little disappointed. "Well that's because we are new," I told him.

So he began to walk with us and was mumbling under his breath, "I can not believe... two white boys... this time of night..." He interrupted himself and scolded us, "What could you be thinking coming out here this time of night? It's dangerous out here." He lectured us for a minute or two that our presence would have only been perceived negatively. We thanked him for the concern but also assured him that we were friends with Jesus and that God himself had our backs.

He nodded in agreement, and we invited him to come with us to get our cold drinks and offered him one too. He agreed, and we walked with him to the store, gave him a Pepsi, and headed back. He told us his name was George but everybody called him 'Geech.' He stayed with us, we didn't really know why but we continued on, mostly in silence. Silence that he broke, by announcing,

"I know I need to get my life right with God."

I acted like I was not surprised by his confession, "Oh?"

"Yeah, I do." He hung his head.

All of the sudden he was not some figure looming in the shadows but I looked into his eyes and I could see that he was a weary man. He wore old jeans and his black shirt was tattered and stained by sweat. He was obviously strung out, hurting for that next high.

He was only thirty (we would find out later) but he looked much older. Something was robbing him of his life, and there did not appear to be much left. I began to feel the compassion of God toward him.

"I am addicted to crack cocaine," he admitted, "and I can't beat it. I been robbin' and runnin' for a week [living on the street] and my life is in shambles."

So there I was, confronted with the reality of the power of the gospel. I looked at him, and in my own human wisdom I feebly responded,

"Have you thought about getting professional help?"

"Yeah, I was in rehab and I flunked out, so now the cops are looking for me and if I go back I will be arrested."

"Oh." I floundered.

I imagine that moment to be something like what a soldier or a police officer that is trained to use a firearm feels. It is not until that moment, where they finally have to draw their weapon and pull the trigger that they find out if they can really do it. I was brutally confronted with the fact that this man's life hung in the balance, that there was no hope for him save that of the gospel and the redemption promised at the cross of Jesus Christ. We knew there was no hope for him except for Jesus.

I had nothing to offer him but Jesus, and I had to pull the trigger. Did I really believe that the gospel was powerful enough for Geech? Did I believe that it could rescue him from crack cocaine? My faith hung in the balance.

I could not use the marketing approach to evangelism. "You have many viable and exciting options open to you good sir, how about trying Jesus? Give him a try for thirty days and if you are not wealthier, smarter, happier, then come back and I will give you a full refund." No, if Geech did not throw his life on the mercies of Jesus, he was going to die. That much was clear.

I turned to him and said, "Do you believe that God has the power to deliver you from drugs?"

And he said, "Oh, man, God's got all the power."

And I said, "That's enough. That's enough faith."

So we brought him into our house, and we talked with him and gave him some food, and we prayed for him, and as God has been known to do, he touched the life of a broken man. God was on the job. I had nothing to tell him, nothing to give him, but Jesus. He listened as we told him about the humble God revealed in Jesus who delighted in exalting the lowly, of the Christ who was himself despised by men, and who came for the sick and not the well.

Geech wept. He had me call his mother to let her know he was alright. She lived right there in the neighborhood, but he could not face her. I spoke with her briefly and asked,

"Would you like Geech, to come home?"

"He knows I want him here, but he won't come," she lamented.

"You love him don't you?" he could hear me.

"God knows I love him." I hung up and pleaded with him,

"Go home to your mother. Don't spend another night on the street." He hung his head and left sadly. Daniel and I prayed again.

I woke up late the next morning to find that Geech had called. We were up late, so Monica (my wife) did not want to wake me. He told her, "You know, they really inspired me last night because they prayed for me, and they walked with me. I am going to turn myself in."

The life of humility and worship is one that is transformed by the power of the gospel. Geech knew that he could not survive an encounter with Jesus and still be the same. We represented Jesus because we offered spiritual life as we walked alongside him. Perhaps it was foolish but we were able show to him the humble Jesus, who would have walked to the BP for his Mountain Dew and would have offered, along the way, deliverance to all who were in bondage. We had nothing and so God was able to be everything.

As it turns out Geech was not wanted by the police. He went to two police stations to turn himself in. They apologized profusely, but explained that they simply did not have a warrant for him, but he could try the station on the other side of town.

Geech's life did not become perfect, but he did get a job and as far as we know he has stayed clean. The life of worship does not have to be perfect—on the contrary, it must acknowledge its imperfection and in so doing realize the strength of God is made perfect in our weakness. While we may not be perfect, we also can not stay the same. It is not business as usual but it is death to the old life and a new life in Christ. Behold "the old has gone and the new has come."[54] A life of worship is a life transformed by the gospel.

chapter 13

a life that imitates Jesus

According to Ephesians 5, it was the whole life of Christ that was a sacrifice to God. Revealing that worship is not one action isolated and distinguished from other more mundane actions. Unfortunately, we too often consider worship as a single discrete action, holy business reserved for Sundays, Easter and Christmas. Please don't misunderstand me; things like singing, dancing, music, prayer and liturgy do characterize the worshiper's life. The life lived in worship and humility, constantly considering the greatness of God, will spontaneously erupt into a variety of declarations of worship.

Our worship life should consist of such things and should be diverse, as diverse as the Bible allows. One can scarcely maintain that they live conscious of the glory of God, in awe of him, if they always worship exactly the same. I truly believe that if you have never wept in the presence of God, then you should desire to see his heart. If you have never fallen on your face with staggering respect and awe for the one who Nahum said "touches the earth and it melts,"[55] then you should ask to see his glory. If you have never lifted up your hands as an act of surrender to God then you should ask to see the cross. If you have never clapped and danced before the King of joy then perhaps you should inquire of the Lord what waits for the people of God in his kingdom. And if you have never stood silently looking on him with the longing of a lover then perhaps you should ask him just how much he loves you.

Discrete moments of worship are important, but they are all expressions, a deeper state of being completely and utterly his, of belonging to God. A life that has been relinquished to God is then free to sing and live and is a sincere expression of the life (which is Christ's) lived as a fragrant offering to God. Romans 12 says it best; "Therefore, I urge you, brothers, in view of God's mercy, to offer your bodies as living sacrifices, holy and pleasing to God—this is your spiritual act of worship."

The call to worship is a call to die and then to be raised with Christ and to truly live. The life of worship imitates Jesus.

chapter **14**

given
completely
to God

Widely regarded as the first Protestant denomination, the Moravians have left a legacy of utter devotion both to God and his cause. After establishing a colony in Bethlehem, Pennsylvania, within a few short years, this tiny community of believers was sending missionaries to ten countries around the world.[56] However, they are most often remembered for their willingness to give their lives completely to God. When faced with the logistical problem of how to reach the slaves in the West Indies with the gospel, the Moravian men sold themselves into slavery in order to be close to those they hoped to reach. They gave up their earthly freedom so the despised of the world might experience eternal relief. No one can say that they did not count the cost. Their only concern was that "the Lamb receives the reward of his suffering."[57] They knew that belonging to Jesus could cost you everything. Jesus all but guaranteed it. *Whoever wants to save his life will lose it, but whoever loses his life for me will save it.*[58]

Jesus did not teach us to compartmentalize our lives. We want to have lives just like everyone else with a little God on Sunday. Please understand that God is awesome. And although he is full of mercy and love toward us, he is not to be trifled with, nor is his cause to be mocked by a life of double mindedness and hypocrisy. These are the snares of the religious. We cannot say that we accept Christ and then go on with our lives unchanged. Important things like our goals, the way we spend money, our time, and how we treat our families, should all be different because we know Jesus.

Tom Sine explains how we are shown a Jesus who is like a life enhancer not a life changer. That he is really just there to help you get up the proverbial mountain faster, to help you on the path that you have set in achieving your goals (the ones you had before Jesus).[59]

That is counter kingdom, a-biblical; it is the timeless human sin of idolatry, reworked for modernity. God is not worshipped and humility is not cultivated in that life. If we want to worship, we must become imitators of the liberator, to become what he would be were he present on your job, in your neighborhood, or with your family. Why would we settle for less? Why would we settle for that tired, pathetic, sin stained paradigm of being human, when God himself has "set an example that you should do as I have done?"[60] God has himself lived the human life so that we could see and imitate. His life was a life of abandon, sacrifice, obedience, self-denial, and worship; it was a life of humility.

Believing that God is worthy of our all, that there is no part of it he is not entitled to, and then responding to that knowledge by relinquishing it to him, is the preeminent act of humility. Humility is the only acceptable posture for worship. God is more glorified by a single act of Christ-like sacrifice than he is by a million dollar cathedral. Have we forgotten the type of life that Jesus lived? Is it so irrelevant to the way his church is to be governed? The world is in a perpetual race to see who can erect the most marvelous building, who can build the most powerful empire. We have followed the fool into his folly. We too have looked to expand the church and even spread the gospel via satellite. God not only wants us to deliver his message but also wants us to look like him as we do it.

The neonizing of God has contributed to our loss of wonder toward him. Not only among us as his people, but also in the world. If we would see his name hallowed and his Kingdom come, we must look to Jesus to not only inform and reform the life of the individual but also the life of Christian institutions. I am jealous for the glory of God to be seen in the world. I am sure that if I see it more clearly I will not be the same. If my family sees him more clearly they will not be the same. My church, my campus, my city are all subject to nothing short of a spiritual revolution if the manifold glory of God is genuinely projected.

The call to worship is a call to remember the deeds of God, his faithfulness, mercy and unfailing love. "Come, let us bow down in worship, let us kneel before the Lord our Maker."[61] Let us begin by remembering the life that never lived a moment outside of perfect submission to the Father. Jesus showed us how to worship God in the life of humility. He showed us how to best glorify him. Once he is established in our mind's eye, let us imitate and re-enact those glorious deeds. Let us clothe ourselves in humility.[62] If we do, the world as we know it will not survive: Maranatha, in us.

PART 3
paradox

It is one of a million wild jests of truth
that we know nothing until we know nothing.
-G.K. Chesterton

chapter 15

the self-
revelation
of God

The world loves heroes. We practically worship them. Heroes reveal a deep-seated lack of contentment about everyday life. We look for someone to do life right, to show us an idealized existence. I recently read an article in the newspaper about an ordinary man who had figured out some extraordinary things about life, and although he was getting press, this man was an unlikely hero. The article began, "He has no training in crisis management. He has never done any counseling. But three times in the past four days, Florida Highway Patrol Trooper, James C. Covert, has managed to talk distraught people out of jumping off the Sunshine Skyway Bridge."[63]

Covert, who does not usually patrol the bridge, happened to be available when the first call came in. The second was a call for a disabled vehicle on the bridge. Of course the vehicle was fine, but the driver was about to jump. At the time the article was published, nine people had already taken their lives that year from that bridge. What was the secret to his unlikely success? The article goes on to say, "The 27-year-old former carpenter says humility and the ability to engage each person in conversation went a long way in helping him prevent three potential suicides."[64] Covert said of his own crisis management tactics, "I assured him I wasn't that brave..."[65]

How do we talk to a world on the brink of destruction? What is the key to reach the world for Jesus? It is humility. This former carpenter got it right. Pride is attractive if I am looking for a conqueror or a tycoon, but the world is only weakened by conquerors. Instead, we are called to be more than that.[66] Humility communicates that I am not better than you, that I can understand. Jesus set for us a model that runs contrary to every worldly pattern of greatness. When I say worldly I do not mean anything outside the church. I mean anything that is not like Jesus. We have adopted plenty of these patterns in our ecclesiastical structures and more importantly, in our personal lives. Jesus not only offers an alternative pattern of thought and action but he offers the fulfillment of life itself.

His paradigm is not easy, nor is it necessarily reasonable, but it is the way of whole and lasting life. His paradigm is a paradox. A paradox is an apparent contradiction that actually reveals a hidden truth. It is often the truest form of truth, something that defies the senses or logic but is deeply profound and meaningfully relevant for that very reason.

This trooper is really a hero because he is doing life right. He is following the lead of the author of life who came to earth to give us a new paradigm for how to live. The problem is that the model is not only an alternative to the status quo, it is completely contrary.

Jesus taught that the least was the most, that to be low was to be nearest to God. He talked of leaders who served and of life found only in death. His take on the world was what Dallas Willard called "the law of inversion,"[67] and what Donald Kraybill called the "upside down Kingdom."[68] The incarnation changed everything.

This chapter is an exploration of the implications of the incarnation.

Certainly, there must be ramifications for God coming in the form he did. The inauspicious birthday of Jesus was just a hint of things to come. His whole life would be lived in humility. The one who could have—should have come in a great display of splendor and Kingly power, chose another way. Let us consider why.

chapter 16
the humility
of God

It might properly be asked whether or not God is even capable of humility. Since God cannot lie, and therefore God must always possess an honest pride in himself, God cannot be confused about the relative merit of himself toward all that is created. He must know that he is, in fact, superior. Yet, Jesus who lowered himself and took on human flesh found in himself the form of a created thing. On what grounds then was Jesus humble? For the answer to that question let us consider the gospel and Jesus' own rationale.

Since true humility, both toward God and others, comes from a divine center, Jesus made the focal point of his life's attention the will of the Father. Consider the profound statements of humility made by Jesus in the gospel of John.

I tell you the truth, the Son can do nothing by himself; he can do only what he sees his Father doing, because whatever the Father does the Son also does.[69]

By myself I can do nothing; I judge only as I hear, and my judgment is just, for I seek not to please myself but him who sent me.[70]

For I have come down from heaven not to do my will but to do the will of him who sent me.[71]

Jesus answered, "My teaching is not my own. It comes from him who sent me.[72]

I am not here on my own, but he who sent me is true. You do not know him,[73]

When you have lifted up the Son of Man, then you will know that I am and that I do nothing on my own but speak just what the Father has taught me.[74]

If God were your Father, you would love me, for I came from God and now am here. I have not come on my own; but he sent me.[75]

I am not seeking glory for myself; but there is one who seeks it, and he is the judge.[76]

The words I say to you are not just my own. Rather, it is the Father, living in me, who is doing his work.[77]

He who does not love me will not obey my teaching. These words you hear are not my own; they belong to the Father who sent me.[78]

Jesus knew who he was, and yet he was showing us, the most unique of all his creation, how we ought to live our lives before God. Jesus demonstrated humility because we needed a demonstration. Jesus humbled himself not because some circumstance dictated it but because it is right for us. Not only was his death a demonstration of his love but his life was as well. His life showed us how to live in intimacy with and worship to the Father. The medium was also the message. The irony is, of course, obvious. He who was without sin was showing us how to live as broken and fallen people. Broken people needed to know how to live before a holy God and his creation. Jesus' incarnation provided that object lesson.

Philippians 2 is the most obvious attempt to describe this radical life paradigm. In this staggering passage, Paul describes the indescribable, chronicling the deity of Christ, and his incredible actions.

He who is the image of the invisible God, the firstborn over all creation, the one for whom all things were created: things in heaven and on earth, visible and invisible, whether thrones or powers or rulers or authorities; all things were created by him and for him, the one who is before all things, and in whom all things hold together, and the one who God was pleased to have all his fullness dwell in, *became nothing.*[79]

He had everything and gave it all up. For what? To become like those he loved. He took the form of those to whom he would bring good news. This is the mystery and the majesty of the incarnation. It is the most profound demonstration of humility imaginable.

Finally, he surrendered to death, the quintessential death of a nobody. This is the paradigm for godliness. Death, however, was not the end. Since Jesus was the embodiment of this principle, because he was the meekest and lowliest man to ever live, because he alone captured the awe of God in the life of humility, not asserting his right to honor and position, He is exalted.[80] All honor and authority is rightfully his.

Everything that he gave up to become our redeemer is returned to him, and the world is left reeling. His work flipped life upside down never to be lived the same again. Happiness, joy, greatness and the knowledge of God, can now only be attained by the path he treads. There is no other way.

Paul writes "therefore." It is because of this unparalleled display of the love of God that he was given back all that was his. Position (v. 9a), prestige (v. 9b), power (v. 10), and prominence (v. 11), all were returned to him. And he deserved it. It means that now "Jesus is Lord." A claim to which James Stewart, the late Scottish professor of theology, asserts is a one of a kind.

> It means the throne of the universe for Christ. It is still a daring claim, as it was at the first, but no one who has honestly faced the fact of Christ can have any doubt at all that the throne is his by right. It has been bought with a price—bought with the hunger in the desert, when he would not make the stones into bread; bought with the tears he shed over the sins of men; bought with the sweat of Gethsemane which was like great drops of blood; bought with the bitter cross where they broke his body in death; bought with the deathless love which through all the years has refused resolutely to let a lost world go. The Captain of the hosts of humanity himself has been in the ranks.[81]

The incarnation changed everything. In retrospect, we can see what Jesus' contemporaries must have had difficulty seeing. That in his abasement he was asserting himself as the greatest man to ever live. Even his closest friends did not seem to know about his divinity. This fact alone is conclusive testimony to the staggering, unsurpassed humility of Jesus. He was God. In the words of the creed, "God of God, light of Light, very God of Very God," "Being of one substance with the Father"[82] and yet he was scarcely recognized as the Messiah. Even that one truth was for him not to be public knowledge.[83]

He was truly the embodiment of this paradox. Jonathan Edwards makes the point better than I can:

> In the person of Christ do meet together infinite glory and lowest humility. Infinite glory, and the virtue of humility, meets in no other person but Christ. They meet in no created person; for no created person has infinite glory, and they meet in no other divine person but Christ. For though the divine nature be infinitely abhorrent to pride, yet humility is not properly predicable of God the Father, and the Holy Ghost, that exist only in the divine nature; because it is a proper excellency only of a created nature; for it consists radically in a sense of a comparative lowness and littleness before God, or the great distance between God and the subject of this virtue; but it would be a contradiction to suppose any such thing in God.[84]

Edwards demonstrates that God abhors pride, but humility is not fitting him since he can not be considered beneath another. Therefore, in his genius, God becomes humbled unto himself. Our redemption comes as a consequence of this divine solution. Christ was able to come under the judgment of God in death and in so doing atone for our sin. However, he also suffered in life. Living as a created thing, in all its limitations, so that we might see the life perfectly lived. I'm saying that God has chosen to give us Jesus, first as a ransom for our sin, but also so that we might know him and his character, so that his life might be re-presented in us. So that we can say with Paul, "I have been crucified with Christ and I no longer live, but Christ lives in me. The life I live in the body, I live by faith in the Son of God, who loved me and gave himself for me."[85] Or even repeat the words of Jesus, "It is the Father, living in me."[86]

John 13 illustrates this clearly. It is a symbolic description of the profound humility we see in the incarnation illustrated by Jesus himself. I wonder what it would have been like to be present at this scene, to have watched the master teacher not only speak the truth to them but to simultaneously dramatize it for them. Jesus himself enacts the paradigm and in so doing displays the "full extent of his love." Verses 3-5 are simply a rewording of Philippians 2.

Jesus knew that the Father had put all things under his power and that he had come from God and was returning to God.

The power, position and identity of Jesus are established. He knows who he is. This is important. Otherwise, it could be said that Jesus might have suffered a mental breakdown. Perhaps he did not have any business on the cross or at the feet of his disciples. John makes certain that we understand that Jesus is in his right mind and at the height of his teaching.

…so he got up from the meal,

As the Master, he would have certainly been sitting at the center, or head, of the table. He was the main attraction; all eyes were on him. He gets up from his place of honor at the table; Jesus initiates, no one comes to him asking him to do it. John 1 tells us that Jesus has ruled from the beginning.[87] To become human, Jesus had to "get up" from his throne.

…took off his outer clothing,

He takes off his priestly garments, his Kingly robes; he strips himself of his very deity.

…and wrapped a towel around his waist.

He then takes the form of a servant putting on, in place of his glory, the flesh of humanity and the rags of a slave. It is this expression of solidarity with the fallen race he has created and for whom he has come to save that allows them to witness then and there the act of redemption...

After that, he poured water into a basin and began to wash his disciples' feet, drying them with the towel that was wrapped around him.

He cleanses us by the blood he shed on the cross. Jesus asks his disciples, he asks us, the same piercing question: "Do you know what I have done for you?" He died and came to life again to remain for all time and all people "teacher and Lord."

Just as Paul exhorted the Philippians to have the same attitude as that of Christ Jesus, Jesus himself leaves this object lesson and labels his own model with these words: "I have set you an example that you should do as I have done to you. I tell you the truth, no servant is greater than his master, nor is a messenger greater than the one who sent him. Now that you know these things, you will be blessed if you do them." Jesus is still the great Rabbi. As James Stewart puts it:

The disciples could never feel that there was anything vague or abstract about his teaching, for it was all being made concrete and personal before their eyes, all incarnate in himself. Was it faith in God that was the lesson? How gloriously he lived that lesson out himself! Was it the forgiving of injuries he was urging upon them? How wholeheartedly he himself forgave! Was it the importance of prayer that he was teaching? He himself prayed all the night long. He did not only speak to them of the necessity of service and self-sacrifice: He took a towel and girded himself and washed their feet. He did not make orations about brotherhood: he went into the homes of the despised, and sat at their tables, and called them friends and brothers. *Christ was the supreme teacher because he lived supremely what he taught, and lived it entirely nonprofessionally and naturally.*

In this he is an example for all his followers forever.[88]

We would not know God, nor would we know how to imitate him if it were not for Jesus. Since and because of the incarnation, all of human life is different. Before his appearing, the best religion was governed by law. It provided mediation between a God who was far off, untouchable, and unknowable. Although we take it for granted and trivialize it by endless trite sayings and little plastic mangers, the incarnation and the expression "the Word became flesh" is beyond the reach of language and human comprehension. The esoteric nature of the incarnation does not alter the truth that now we have knowledge of Him. "No one has ever seen God, but God the One and only, who is at the Father's side, has made him known."[89] We know Jesus.

John begins his first epistle with these words: "That which was from the beginning, which we have heard, which we have seen with our eyes, which we have looked at and our hands have touched--this we proclaim concerning the Word of life."[90] It was not until after he was gone that John realized the implications of the friendship he had with Jesus. You can almost hear him reveal in the sensual experience of knowing Jesus, whom he had heard, seen and touched.

Jesus is the greatest pedagogical gesture from the greatest teacher in the universe; his incarnation is God's object lesson about himself and the perfect human life. Jesus is the self-revelation of God to us.

If Jesus had not revealed God to us, how would we regard God? Any conception of God without Jesus is not God at all. Perhaps we would know him as, what C.S. Lewis calls "a cosmic bell hop,"[91] who comes running to grant our every wish and who is thankful for the tips we give him. So some say. Perhaps we would know him as an angry God, a "cosmic sadist,"[92] who delights in the torment of his creation. So some say. Perhaps we would simply know him as a distant God, unapproachable, inaccessible, cold and unconcerned with my insignificant life. So I might say, if it were not for the revelation of Jesus.

This is an anthropomorphic view of God. It is the attempt to construct a human God. To create God in our image based on what we know about human behavior and characteristics. We magnify those traits to divine proportions. This was the folly of the Greeks, whose gods were even more whimsical than the people they ruled over. While we were busy constructing a human conception of God, God was busy becoming human and at once answered our deepest questions--for those who are interested in the answer. Two thousand years later no one in history can match the moral integrity or even popular regard of this man from Nazareth.

Even in the minds of unbelievers he is unapproached by rival, would be saviors. No other man, or woman, or institution can compare with the effect that Jesus has had on history, and no one else continues to capture the imaginations of all who hear of him. "There is no one else," said a prominent Hindu to Stanley Jones, "who is seriously bidding for the heart of the world except Jesus Christ? There is no one else on the field."[93]

So who has Jesus revealed God to be? And in turn, who are we to be as we re-present God to an unbelieving world? Brace yourself: a servant. Humility characterizes our King, and we his subjects honor him as we imitate him.

He is the most perplexing and fabulous personality in our history. He is God become man...and the contrast is suddenly startling, the paradox gripping. Consider the revealed character of God. From Jesus' life we learn that God is, meek and glorious, austere and approachable, compassionate and just, loving and honest, a visionary and a realist, a servant and a king.

This is the gospel. Has it changed your life yet? Are you different from the hearing of it? Does your heart burn as it is retold? Jesus is the same. He is still compelling, but our re-presentation of him is often weakened by our strength as we look to pyrotechnics, video projections, gold alters, state of the art preachers in $900 suits to communicate the truth about the humble Jesus. No wonder people misunderstand. Thomas A Kempis imagines what Jesus would say. "I became the most humble and the lowest of all men, that you might overcome your pride with my humility."[94] Paul, who had not walked with Jesus, understood this about his master. He wrote,

> When I came to you, brothers, I did not come with eloquence or superior wisdom as I proclaimed to you the testimony about God. For I resolved to know nothing while I was with you except Jesus Christ and him crucified. I came to you in weakness and fear, and with much trembling. My message and my preaching were not with wise and persuasive words, but with a demonstration of the Spirit's power, so that your faith might not rest on men's wisdom, but on God's power.[95]

Let us dedicate ourselves to the passionate re-telling, re-presenting of his story with our mouths and with our lives, to live the incarnational life and make his story ours.

self-denial

*For seeing it is a holy exercise both for men to humble themselves,
and confess their humility, why should we in similar necessity
use this less than did those of old?*
John Calvin

chapter 17

denying
yourself

Some have argued that a culture is defined by its use of language. In other words, we are what we say (speech act theory).[97] Some linguists argue that language's centrality to social activity can not be understated. At the very least, you can tell a lot about a culture by what they say or more to the point, what they don't say. The use of language is the most basic and pervasive form of human interaction. Meaning, of course, is the key. There is nothing significant about the stringing together of arbitrary phonemes to signify something or another. What is important is what those sounds mean to the individual or society.

To this point, I have deliberately not defined the word humility. When a word is meant to symbolize not just an object or even an abstract concept, a definition helps to contain it, given the referent limits and boundaries, so that it can be easily identified and effectively used. Here that is not entirely helpful. I am contending that humility is more than a word. It is a virtue. More than that, it is the chief virtue exhibited in the life of Jesus. Because that is my contention, it is more important to explore humility than to define it. For it has no limits, no boundaries to discover and to artificially create them would be to misunderstand, and in the final estimation, misrepresent humility.

Language can be a tricky thing. As I have thought further about this subject, even while writing about it, I have found that in my life there has been a revival of sorts in my use of certain words. At first it seemed as though the terminology was archaic and outdated, I sounded like a monk to myself. However, I have come to realize that this language is really quite biblical and perhaps its absence reflects something about our collective state of mind.

chapter **18**

deifying
the self

Whatever happened to words like renunciation, modesty, contrition, self-denial, subjection and abasement? Humility, which I obviously consider a positive human quality, in its most common derivation, humiliation, has come to represent the most heinous and de-humanizing of all acts. To apply the term nothing, or nothingness, to oneself is popularly regarded as a cardinal sin. This view however, was not shared by Abraham,[98] Job,[99] Paul,[100] or even Jesus.[101] Certainly, Abraham, Paul and especially Jesus were more than nothing. Yet, their willingness to identify with the term is evidence of their thoughts about God, themselves and others. Our unwillingness to do the same also reveals something about us as a culture. Just as the use of the term reflects their uncompromising humility, which is the secret to the exalted spiritual life, perhaps its absence in our usage reflects our spiritual futility. Since when have we heard and embraced words like Thomas A Kempis',

> Is it such a great matter if you, who are but dust and nothingness, subject yourself to man for the sake of God, when I, the all-powerful, the Most High, Who created all things out of nothing, humbly subjected myself to man for your sake? I became the most humble and the lowest of all men that you might overcome your pride with my humility. Learn to obey, you who are but dust! Learn to humble yourself, you who are but earth and clay, and bow down under the foot of every man! Learn to break your own will, to submit to all subjection! Be zealous against yourself! Allow no pride to dwell in you, but prove yourself so humble and lowly that all may walk over you and trample upon you as dust in the streets! What have you, vain man, to complain of? What answer can you make, vile sinner, to those who accuse you, you who have so often offended God and so many times deserved hell?[102]

These words are hard; they certainly rail against the present current of teaching about the self. What words then have we substituted in their place? What is important to us? The greatest indictment is that all of our buzzwords today could begin and end with self. Our language seems to encourage us to be self-actualized, self-motivated, self-esteemed, self-realized and self-helped. Instead of renunciation, we say actualization; instead of being modest, we are proud; not contrite but assertive; in place of self-denial we are encouraged to be self-satisfied; never self-abased we are self-esteemed; instead of being subject to another, we are empowered to self-realization. And the prophets turn in their graves as men say to us, "Where is your God!"[103] It seems we have lost him in the crowd of ourselves.

Even in John Wesley's time the popular sentiment was the same, and his advice sound.

Reject with horror that favorite maxim of the old Heathen, sprung from the bottomless pit, Tanti eris aliis, quanti tibi fueris: 'The more you value yourself, the more others will value you.' Not so; on the contrary, both God and man 'resist the proud:' and, as 'God giveth grace to the humble,' so humility, not pride, recommends us to the esteem and favor of men, especially those that fear God."[104]

Our problem is that we do not know how to reconcile weakness with success. It simply does not register as a possibility in our minds. Which is all the more reason why we can no longer be conformed to the pattern of this world, but we must be transformed by the renewing of our minds.[105] Humility is first a state of mind, and second, a way of life. The modern idol is the self, and we must deny it the worship and attention it craves. Self-denial is the daily business of those who would be humble. There is no other way. Jesus did not leave another option.

All three of the synoptic gospels, in a rare expression of linguistic solidarity, transcribe Jesus' words without the slightest deviation. There is little doubt that all of those who first followed Jesus knew what we do not: "If anyone would come after me, he *must deny himself* and take up his cross and follow me."[106] He must deny himself; there simply is no other way to come after, to follow Jesus. I can not make this point emphatically enough.

chapter 19

living a
contradiction

Some have recently concocted the notion that in this life following
Jesus will mean material success, wealth and prosperity. Nothing
could be further from what Jesus promised. In another place he said,
"You will have trouble."[107] Don't get me wrong, Jesus also says of his
commands, "You are blessed if you do them."[108] But the blessing that
is promised is not freedom from trouble or persecution, but freedom
from the tyranny of the self. Under God's leadership, we are no longer
slaves to sin, but we are free to be utterly his. We can not exchange the
scepter of sin for the headship of self. God is our reward. He does not
promise wealth or material prosperity. I defy you to find that in the
teaching or life of Jesus.

The other day I was driving on the interstate and a big car caught
my attention. I say caught, but this car really demanded my attention.
I could not help but admire the car from a distance in all its opulence.

It was sort of like how I imagine the Taj Mahal to be, overwhelmingly gaudy, more like an attraction than a place to live. It was a brand new white Cadillac; the windows were completely darkened (even the windshield). It had solid gold detailing and lights around the license plate. My admiration turned to contempt as I thought of this icon of the vain, hollow human pursuits of our day and the lie that material things bring contentment and reflect importance. I was surprised to see what looked like a blue sticker of some kind on the trunk. Why would you put a sticker on a car like that? I pulled closer only to be mortified by what the sticker said: "Clergy."

We are to be people of contrast, great in our service, humble in our leadership, and rich in our giving. But I do not believe this is the kind of contrast that Jesus had in mind. Do our lives reflect the humble life of Christ? While this story illustrates the implicit contradiction of Christian luxury, it also illustrates my own lack of humility. When it comes to sin all of us have areas of minimized weakness. That is, while we are equal to the vilest sinner in variety, frequency and duration of sin, we will invariably find something with which we do not struggle (or at least are in fervent denial of it). We then proceed to judge everyone else on that highly subjective (and I might add convenient) basis.

At the time, I drove a little Toyota with no air-conditioning so I felt I could judge this guy. It does not mean that what I observed was okay, but in that moment I realized I was no different. I sensed the Lord asking me, "How does your life misrepresent me?" More than one thing came to mind. It's easy to see judgmentalism and pride in others, it is so very obvious. Yet, it is conspicuously absent in our own times of introspection. Curious, don't you think? Nothing is so difficult to detect in ourselves because nothing is so deep rooted. A helpful hint: if you are feeling self-righteous, you are wrong. If you are feeling superior to another, you are not. We let others down. We demonstrate hypocrisy, and we contradict our teacher. We say, "I'm only human, give me a break." But when it comes to the shortcomings of others, we say, "They should know better."

What Jesus taught and demonstrated was how to deny yourself and in the process receive eternal life and everlasting joy in the presence of the Father. Soon enough we will receive the reward for our suffering, but for now suffering and the character to endure and not elude it is our crown.[109] It is the badge that we wear that identifies us to the world that we are followers of the Lamb. Jesus was lowly, so we must be lowly. No greater act of self-denial has ever been performed than the sacrifice of the cross. We follow the Lamb of God.

The bad news is that if we continue to live for our own development and our own fulfillment, if we continue to exalt the "self," God will tip the scales against us. The good news is that once we have embraced self-denial, just as personally, God will exalt. "Come near to God and he will come near to you. Wash your hands, you sinners, and purify your hearts, you double-minded. Grieve, mourn and wail. Change your laughter to mourning and your joy to gloom. Humble yourselves before the Lord, and he will lift you up."[110] The same passage from Thomas A. Kempis that I cited earlier concludes with these words:

> But my eye has spared you because your soul was precious in my sight, so that you might know my love and always be thankful for my benefits, so that you might give yourself continually to true subjection and humility, and might patiently endure contempt.[111]

I know that we have problems, that we do underestimate our worth in Christ, that people struggle with a proper image of themselves (although it's usually too high). Death to the emphasis on the self, with all its problems, will mean life to the soul. "For if you live according to the sinful nature, you will die; but if by the Spirit you put to death the misdeeds of the body, you will live."[112] "For Christ died for sins once for all, the righteous for the unrighteous, to bring you to God. He was put to death in the body but made alive by the Spirit."[113] The soul after all, is what will endure.

Please don't misunderstand me. I am not implying that people should live in guilt or self-loathing. I do realize that in our time we seem to have made considerable progress in dealing with guilt and shame which is no more from God than hypocrisy and pride. But what if in the process of imparting words of life about the work of Jesus and the worth of those who bear his image, we have simply exchanged one malady, a kind of self-loathing, for another more potentially destructive, self-love. If self-respect or self-esteem is gained at the cost of humility then it is too high a price. What guilt and shame does to the physical life, pride does to the spiritual. If you have to suffer one malady, may it be the former.

chapter 20

embracing the truth

True humility is sober. As I have discussed previously, Jesus knew who he was, and he lived humbly. He willingly denied himself giving up his position, his rights. This of course brought him the deepest joy. "For the joy set before him [he] endured the cross, scorning its shame."[114] The admonition of Paul is not to consider yourself "more highly than you ought."[115] Self-denial does not mean denying your worth as a child of God or a bearer of his image. It does mean the sacrifice of the rights that a child of God is entitled to. Self-denial requires sober judgment that neither elevates nor denigrates oneself. As I have said before, humility is the grace of self-forgetting. To focus on yourself in your superiority *or* inferiority is to miss the point of humility. Humility is simply not concerned with the self at all. God will take care of you. If we learn to live as Jesus did, preferring others, then we will experience the joy he did. We will scorn the shame that accompanies such self-denial and ultimately, in the death of ourselves, we will receive life in him.

Self-denial sometimes means depriving yourself of good things. Some years ago I was in Mexico City with a team of students. We were there for a workshop on missions. It was there that I met Saul and Pilar Cruz, two of the most remarkable people I know. They are both incredibly talented and caring, with outstanding credentials. They wear their success so lightly that it draws people to them. Seeing humility in such people is like stopping to appreciate a cool breeze, or like listening to good music. It sets the soul at ease. It was our privilege to learn from them and work at their side in their fully indigenous work known as Armonia. However, the clearest and most powerful lesson was not at all a part of the curriculum. It was their lives.

It is rare to meet someone who immediately makes you think of Jesus. It is that way with Saul. Saul, who holds a Ph.D., has chosen to give his life and ministry for the poorest of the poor in Mexico City. When we arrived, Paco, a co-laborer with the Cruz's met us at the airport and informed us there had been a fire in one of the villages. All night they had stayed up with the people as the fire ravaged their homes. It was Saul who would find the bodies of a mother and two of her four children, charred beyond recognition. Paco informed us that because of this tragedy it was not likely we would see much of Saul and Pilar that week. Fortunately, Saul did make time for us. In between writing requests to the government for relief aid for the 800 families who were now homeless and helping the men sort through the rubble for any remaining valuables, he led us in a Bible study of Matthew 9 and explained that Jesus came to bring life to the whole person.

Jesus can too give life to the spiritual, intellectual and physical body. I could not help but notice that Saul wore the grace of humility with honor. He knew that he was living the life of his savior, and it obviously gave him joy.

A few of us went with Saul and Pilar to the wake of the mother and her children who had died in the fire. It was there that I saw Jesus most clearly. This was a funeral of the poor; no politicians were present, no foreign missionaries, no government officials, just the poor...and Saul. Although he did not know the bereaved family prior to the fire, Saul and Pilar had gone to help them find shelter and to give them comfort. We picked up the widower and the two surviving daughters, who had escaped the fire with her newborn sister.

Everything about the funeral was foreign to us. We were having trouble making sense of it. There were hundreds of people gathered around the grave sites and the wooden caskets, two of which were very small, lay at the center of the crowd. Saul was weaving in and out of the crowd. There was constant crying, but when the weeping of the oldest daughter became noticeably labored, Saul moved toward her. He got hold of a bag and as Pilar held her, he tried to get her to breathe into the bag. As the funeral ended, the girl would not leave the graveside, and it was Saul and Pilar who carried her away. We all stood and prayed and took it in. But as I remember that day it is Christ that is glorified in my mind.

What I mean is that I could have taken anyone in the world with a rudimentary knowledge of whom Jesus was and asked her to identify the person in this crowd who most resembles him, and there would have been no dispute. The character of Christ is punctuated by self-denial. Those who would be like him will stand out of the crowd. All the time I spent in Mexico City only confirms what I saw that day. Whenever someone was in need, Saul was there. It was as though his life meant nothing. In the short time we were with them, they went without sleep, food, rest and support. All of which were good things, but not as good as imitating their King. That is why Paul said; "Now I rejoice in what was suffered for you, and I fill up in my flesh what is still lacking in regard to Christ's afflictions, for the sake of his body."[116]

The Cruz's knew that in self-denial they complete what is lacking in Christ's afflictions. Not to say that his atonement was insufficient, it was not. What remains is the re-presentation of those afflictions to the world. This is the noble and glorious task of his people for the sake of those who would be his body. "Here is a trustworthy saying: If we died with him, we will also live with him; if we endure, we will also reign with him."[117] Saul and Pilar were not afraid to deny themselves. Or maybe they were afraid but they trusted the words of Jesus enough to do it anyway.

They seemed to live in such a way that disregarded themselves, not devaluing their own lives, not overestimating their value; it was as if they forgot to estimate it. They lived in the truth about the greatness of the way of Jesus. They knew they were loved by God and could therefore offer love unconditionally to others. It was the sober embrace of the truth. We too must learn to understand that our lives are hidden with Christ in God. That our true status is as kings and priests to our God, and the height of that position allows us unheard of freedom to humble ourselves and to experience the joy of living as Jesus did. We are liberated by the truth of God's unbelievable love for us, so that we can starve our hungry egos in favor of those who will die without the nourishment that we have found.

Humility is not possible without self-denial. Any version that proposes differently is a counterfeit virtue. Chesterton argued that modern humility is not absent just misplaced. We do, today, have a version of humility, but it has nothing to do with self-denial and it certainly does not have a divine center. No, Chesterton writes,

> Modesty has moved from the organ of ambition. Modesty has settled on the organ of conviction; where it was never meant to be. A man was meant to be doubtful about himself but undoubting about the truth; this has been exactly reversed.[118]

His point is that when it comes to pride in personal achievement, resolve, or even moral integrity we are the boldest prognosticators of our own goodness. Personal modesty has lost its charm, and we would rather believe that virtually anything we think or theorize is true, simply because we thought it. This is, after all, the basis of moral relativism. Although the individual is always right, we are not supposed to believe that another may be wrong or that any conviction with universal qualities is possible.

Relativism has created a sort of "humility of reason." Where we should distrust ourselves, we have full confidence. Where we should trust reason or revelation, we exercise a kind of intellectual agnosticism. True humility requires self-denial not truth denial.

chapter 21
believable
truth

Godly denial must be wrapped in sobriety. Scripture is clear that we are to take up our cross and deny ourselves, and yet Jesus was just as clear that "whoever disowns me before men, I will disown him before my Father in heaven."[119] Truth transcends the individual, and while humility is essential in the implementation and explanation of truth, (because we are fallible and given to bias), that truth itself is not subject to anyone, and it is not ours to deny. It is possible to be humble and also be a person of conviction. It is the way one communicates and ultimately lives out those convictions that must be governed by humility.

Self-denial, then, is a megaphone for the truth. If we are willing to deny ourselves for what is true, then the world will notice. If we use the truth only for our gain, then who can be expected to believe?

It may be that those who preach on television and ask for my money are in fact telling the truth, yet I am inclined to disbelieve them because of the obvious advantage to them.

In a poll I read some years ago, Americans related a list of the top twenty occupations that we most admire. In addition, a top twenty list was complied resulting in the "America's sleaziest ways to make a living."[120] TV evangelist appears third on the second list. The only occupation considered sleazier? "Drug dealer" and "organized crime boss." It was not, however, considered more nefarious than "prostitute" and "rock and roll star."[121] Is it really any wonder why? People will not believe us about the truth of the gospel, or anything else for that matter, if we use it for our own advancement.[122] Such spiritual opportunists do more harm than good for the gospel and the Kingdom of God.

Paul once argued vehemently that those who served God in the ministry should not have to work and that they were worthy of a salary.[123] Yet, he did not avail himself of that right simply because he wanted those he served to know that he did it for Jesus and no other reason. His claim to apostleship was never so strong, and his ministry unprecedented because he lived a life denying himself, a life that imitated his master. He gave those who had never seen Jesus a life-sized example of what he was like. So much so that he could say under inspiration, "Imitate me as I imitate Christ."[124] The fact that he was whipped, beaten, jailed and constantly under the threat of death is precisely what made his message credible and his motive clear. Time has passed but this principle remains the same.

The power of the gospel is foolishness to those who are perishing because those who are perishing chase after worldly power. Their search for immortality is in vain. The way of the gospel is the way of the cross and for those who come to die, it is life. The paradox only provides credibility because the world is looking for what it has been promised, but (outside of Jesus) has never been delivered: that is redemption.

chapter **22**

the power
of self-denial

Self-denial and humility are not synonymous. Self-denial can often attract great attention to itself, which, as I have said, is perilous to budding humility. Thus, the denial of the self, alone, does not produce humility. The ascetics, while impressive, were not living the model of Jesus. He gave his life freely, but Jesus did not kill himself. It is not a virtue to look for ways to deprive yourself of something good just to attain humility. Again, this is only a more subtle self-centeredness. Humility never draws attention to itself. Acts of self-denial will characterize humility, and the virtue cannot be attained without it. However, humility demands denial for the sake of another. Denial, in a vacuum, or for no reason (i.e. the ascetics), is masochism. Christ-like self-denial is for the sake of another. I explore this principle further in chapter five.

Anything that is unexpected is going to attract attention. If the norm in a restaurant is to sit in chairs, and I enter, thank the waiter for my menu and then proceed to sit on the floor, I will attract attention. In a world that is full of individuals who are wired to prioritize self-preservation above all else, those who would deny themselves will attract attention. Sacrifice always helps a cause.

In the early church those who were martyred became heroes, and for a short period of time, Christians were actually turning themselves in to be killed. While that probably misses the spirit of self-sacrifice, one can not help but be moved by the abandon of self-regard for the sake of the cause. Like kamikaze pilots, whose motivation no one knows but whose conviction is indelibly asserted by their sacrifice, self-denial commands attention.

I have always loved the story of Polycarp, the Bishop of Antioch. The second century document known as the Martyrdom of Polycarp chronicles his last days. He was a bishop over the churches in Smyrna at the time, and when it came to his attention that he was wanted by the local authorities, he gave himself to prayer. In this time of prayer he fell into a trance that lasted three days. In it, he received a vision of his pillow burning. Once he awoke, he understood that he was to be burned alive. When the men came to get him, he did not run or hide. He invited them in and prepared a meal for them. While they ate he asked if he could have one hour to pray, and they agreed. I have included most of that short record compiled by eyewitnesses.

> But when at length he brought his prayer to an end, after remembering all who at any time had come in his way, small and great, high and low, and all the universal Church throughout the world, the hour of departure being come, they seated him on an ass and brought him into the city, it being a high Sabbath. And he was met by Herod the captain of police and his father Nicetes, who also removed him to their carriage and tried to prevail upon him, seating themselves by his side and saying, 'Why what harm is there in saying, Caesar is Lord,

and offering incense, with more to this effect, 'and saving thyself?' But he at first gave them no answer. When however they persisted, he said, 'I am not going to do what ye counsel me.' Then they, failing to persuade him, uttered threatening words and made him dismount with speed, so that he bruised his shin, as he got down from the carriage. And without even turning round, he went on his way promptly and with speed, as if nothing had happened to him, being taken to the stadium; there being such a tumult in the stadium that no man's voice could be so much as heard. But as Polycarp entered into the stadium, a voice came to him from heaven; 'Be strong, Polycarp, and play the man.' And no one saw the speaker, but those of our people who were present heard the voice. And at length, when he was brought up, there was a great tumult, for they heard that Polycarp had been apprehended. When then he was brought before him, the proconsul enquired whether he were the man. And on his confessing that he was, he tried to persuade him to a denial saying, 'Have respect to thine age,' and other things in accordance therewith, as it is their wont to say; 'Swear by the genius of Caesar; repent and say, Away with the atheists.' Then Polycarp with solemn countenance looked upon the whole multitude of lawless heathen that were in the stadium, and waved his hand to them; and groaning and looking up to heaven he said, 'Away with the atheists.' But when the magistrate pressed him hard and said, 'Swear the oath, and I will release thee; revile the Christ,' Polycarp said, 'Fourscore and six years have I been His servant, and He hath done me no wrong. How then can I blaspheme my King who saved me?' But on his persisting again and saying, 'Swear by the genius of Caesar,' he answered, 'If thou supposest vainly that I will swear by the genius of Caesar, as thou sayest, and feignest that thou art ignorant who I am, hear thou plainly, I am a Christian. But if thou wouldest learn the doctrine of Christianity, assign a day and give me a hearing.' The proconsul said; 'Prevail upon the people.' But Polycarp said; 'As for thyself, I should have held thee worthy of discourse; for we have been taught to render, as is meet, to princes and authorities appointed by God such honor as does us no harm; but as for these, I do not hold them worthy, that I should defend myself before them.' Whereupon the proconsul said; 'I have wild beasts here and I will throw thee to them, except thou repent' But he said, 'Call for them: for the repentance from better to worse is a change not permitted to us; but it is a noble thing to change from untowardness to righteousness' Then he said to him again, 'I will cause thee to be consumed by fire, if thou despisest the wild beasts, unless thou repent.' But Polycarp said; 'Thou threatenest that fire which burneth for a season and after a little while is quenched: for thou art ignorant of the fire of the future judgment and eternal punishment, which is reserved for the ungodly. But why delayest thou? Come, do what thou wilt.' Saying these things and more besides, he was inspired with courage and joy, and his countenance was filled with grace, so that not only did it not drop in dismay at the things which were said to him, but on the contrary the proconsul was astounded and sent his own herald to proclaim three times in the midst of the stadium, 'Polycarp hath confessed himself to be a Christian.' When this was proclaimed by the herald, the whole multitude both of Gentiles and of Jews who dwelt in Smyrna cried out with ungovernable wrath and with a loud shout, 'This is the teacher of Asia, the father of the Christians, the puller down of our gods, who teacheth numbers not to sacrifice nor worship.' Saying these things, they shouted aloud and asked the Asiarch Philip to let a lion loose upon Polycarp. But he said that it was not lawful for him, since he had brought the sports to a close. Then they thought fit to shout out with one accord that Polycarp should be burned alive. For it must needs be that the matter of the vision should be fulfilled, which was shown him concerning his pillow, when he saw it on fire while praying, and turning round he said prophetically to the faithful who were with him, 'I must needs be burned alive.' These things then happened with so great speed, quicker than words could tell, the crowds forthwith collecting from the workshops and baths timber and faggots, and the Jews more especially assisting in this with zeal, as is their wont. But when the pile was made ready, divesting himself of all his upper garments and loosing his girdle, he endeavored also to take off his shoes, though not in the habit of doing this before, because all the faithful at all times vied eagerly who should soonest touch his flesh. For he had been treated with all honor for his holy life even before his gray hairs came. Forthwith then the instruments that were prepared for the pile were placed about him; and as they were going likewise to nail him to the stake, he said; 'Leave me as I am; for He that hath granted me to endure the fire will grant me also to remain at the pile unmoved, even without the security which ye seek from the nails.' So they did not nail him, but tied him. Then he, placing his hands behind him and being bound to the stake, like a noble ram out of a great flock for an offering, a burnt sacrifice made ready and acceptable to God, looking up to heaven said; 'O Lord God Almighty, the Father of Thy beloved and blessed Son Jesus Christ, through whom we have received the knowledge of Thee, the God of angels and powers and of all creation and of the whole race of the righteous, who live in Thy presence; I bless Thee for that Thou hast granted me this day and hour, that I might receive a portion amongst the number of martyrs in the cup of [Thy] Christ unto resurrection of eternal life, both of soul and of body, in the incorruptibility of the Holy Spirit. May I be received among these in Thy presence this day, as a rich and acceptable sacrifice, as Thou didst prepare and reveal it beforehand, and hast accomplished it, Thou that art the faithful and true God. For this cause, yea and for all things, I praise Thee, I bless Thee, I glorify Thee, through the eternal and heavenly High-priest, Jesus Christ, Thy beloved Son, through whom with Him and the Holy Spirit be glory both now [and ever] and for the ages to come. Amen.' When he had offered up the Amen and finished his prayer, the firemen lighted the fire. And, a mighty flame flashing forth, we to whom it was given to see, saw a marvel, yea and we were preserved that we might relate to the rest what happened. The fire, making the appearance of a vault, like the sail of a vessel filled by the wind, made a wall round about the body of the martyr; and it was there in the midst, not like flesh burning, but like [a loaf in the oven or like] gold and silver refined in a furnace. For we perceived such a fragrant smell, as if it were the wafted odor of frankincense or some other precious spice. So at length the lawless men, seeing that his body could not be consumed by the fire, ordered an executioner to go up to him and stab him with a dagger. And when he had done this, there came forth [a dove and] a quantity of blood, so that it extinguished the fire; and all the multitude marveled that there should be so great a difference between the unbelievers and the elect.[125]

Can that be said of us? What was different about Polycarp was his obvious disregard for his own life? What should have been irresistible power of coercion held by the emperor's guard, the power of life and death, was reduced to nothing before the power of self-denial. Polycarp's life was his, his to give. Although Polycarp was killed, his death was, without a doubt, a victory for the church and his martyrdom would become an amazing source of courage and resolve among the followers of Christ to this day. Polycarp knew the truth about Jesus, and he lived and even died imitating it. So that in his death, as in his life, testimony was given to the power of Jesus.

Instead of its mockery, all who were present saw the majesty of the cross. Jesus gave all that he had and calls for his followers to do nothing less to attain the pearl of life. The fifth century monastic John Cassian wrote,

> Humility cannot possibly be acquired without giving up everything: and as long as a man is a stranger to this, he cannot possibly attain the virtue of obedience, or the strength of patience, or the serenity of kindness, or the perfection of love; without which things our hearts cannot possibly be a habitation for the Holy Spirit: as the Lord says through the prophet: 'Upon whom shall My spirit rest, but on him that is humble and quiet and hears My words,'[126]

There are countless examples in history of people who have radically denied themselves and have consequently changed the world around them. One more modern illustration of the power of self-denial would be the civil rights movement of the 1960s.

There were two emblematic voices in the civil rights movement. Both were competing for the minds of America, black and white. Martin Luther King Jr. was the champion of non-violence. His campaign was riddled with tears, heartache and loss. Malcolm X criticized this approach saying it was destined to fail and repeated the words of Karl Marx, "There can be no revolution without bloodshed."[127] But as King and those who fought with the weapon of non-violence knew all too well, their revolution was in fact born in bloodshed, but instead of the blood of their enemies, it was their own blood they offered for the sake of the cause.[128]

King knew and preached the power of self-denial. In the face of an oppressive system, people marched and were beaten, and as dogs and fire hoses ripped into the flesh of children, America watched and was wooed by the moral strength of non-violence. It was on the back of the respect earned by the non-violent movement that the alternative voice, a voice for power, was heard. Men like Stokely Carmichael, Huey Newton and Malcolm X were all correct when they called a racist system and racist people to account. Their demands for representation in government, employment opportunities, access to housing and education, and their plea for power to be given to the people, were just. But this was not the voice that began to melt the cold hearts of hatred and racism in this country.

It was the corporate practice of self-denial that captivated the world. It was when rural residents stood in line all day under threat of violence just to vote. It was when men and women boycotted the bus system and walked to work, sometimes as much as eight miles a day for months, to protest bus segregation that won the watching world. They were being jailed, and beaten and even murdered and not fighting back. Even the most jaded and racially divided country could not stand up to such a display of raw spiritual power.

While others were calling for retribution, which was their right, King made his stand according to the unlikely battle plan of Jesus and waged a war of love, "to save the soul of a nation."[129] What is more revolutionary than loving your enemies? Combating the hatred of another with the boundless love of God? Like King, Ghandi too applied the Sermon on the Mount and realized in some small way the wisdom of the greatest sermon ever preached.[130] And like Abraham Lincoln concluded, "Do I not destroy my enemy when I make him my friend?"[131]

Self-denial can resurrect a dead world. Jesus himself would submit to the Father in his death, "not my will but yours."[132] His self-denial would mean our ultimate liberation. Where people have imitated this enigmatic truth, they have triumphed. Paul preached the same message saying, "Do not repay evil for evil but overcome evil with good."[133] King died believing that the way of the cross and the way of self-denial was the way to freedom, not only for himself but also for his nation. He would give all he had and become a symbol of that which he preached. We then, like the writers of the Polycarp's tale, conclude:

For him, being the Son of God, we adore, but the martyrs as disciples and imitators of the Lord we cherish, as they deserve for their matchless affection towards their own King and Teacher. May it be our lot also to be found partakers and fellow-disciples with them.[134]

PART 5
others

When he saw them, he hurried from the entrance of his tent to meet them and bowed low to the ground.
-Genesis 18:2

chapter **23**

the holy
other

I said earlier that humility requires a change of mind, a new way of thinking, about God, yourself and others. Any argument for a divine center to life is not likely to instigate much opposition from Christians. Yet, the next step toward humility and the imitation of Jesus, the elevation of others, might. This chapter is meant as an apologetic for the spiritual and personal significance of others in our lives. Giving the other a specific name is not going to be possible. Simply put, the other is anyone who is neither God nor you, specifically someone who is in need, someone who is poor.

Even though these people are themselves sinners, because of their spiritual significance for those who come in contact with them, they are holy. God has chosen to affiliate himself with the needy, making them holy by association. Any interaction that ensues is an interaction with the holy. If we respond with disdain or even indifference, we have insulted the holiness of God. This is, in part, why the anger of God burns against those that would oppress and trample the weak because it is not just a travesty of justice, but it is an indirect form of blasphemy. For those of us who are content to be humble before God, in response to his obvious holiness, it behooves us to understand the biblical association of others with the holiness of God. To others, we bear that image as well. In one moment, a friend or a stranger in need confronts me, and that person is the holy other for me. In the next moment, I am in need, and I am representsing that to my friend or that stranger.

One recent Christmas Eve I took my family out for a dinner. The only restaurant we could find open was a Denny's which I knew would cost a little more than I had hoped to spend. I quietly asked the kids (remember I have six) to just get water in order to save some money. I was not worried about it, but Christmas can be expensive.

As we were finishing our grand slams, the waitress came over to us to report, "Your bill has been picked up by the gentleman at the register." I was confused. I have never had a stranger do something like that for me. Maybe because it was also for my wife and children, I was really touched. We all walked over to him (surprise spoiled) and thanked him. I am still not sure why he did it. He only said, "Merry Christmas. Enjoy your family." What I do know is that what he did was Holy. I don't know if he was a believer or not, but I do know that our family represented the presence of God for him, and that gesture (although not morally required) was worship to God.

chapter 24

his image

The first chapter of Genesis establishes that human beings are vastly different from all the other creatures of God's creation. Created on the last day, we bear his image. That alone is indisputable grounds for the dignity of all people. However, sin grew and developed sophisticated structures and systems favoring some and not others. Our history is a pitiful expose on our inability to realize the dignity of all people. The promise to Abraham was that he would be a blessing to all the nations, and Jesus, his seed, would fulfill that promise and prove, once and for all that God's love transcends the racial, economic, lingual and cultural divisions that we have created to deprive some of their dignity. Jesus broke down the dividing wall of hostility and made the two into one.[136] The result was an affirmation of the value of all the peoples of the world.

On a global level all people bear the divine image, and yet we have so tarnished it that it is barely recognizable. We are not struck, at first glance, by the image of the invisible God on the face of everyday people. We are given to judgment. We misunderstand, and from our misunderstanding, we group and categorize so that we can justify our mistrust and eventually our mistreatment of others. Consider how we drive.

The most handsome spiritual life often becomes disfigured and unrecognizable in traffic. Anyone who cuts us off or drives too slow (that's what gets to me), or forgets to signal, or makes any number of mistakes that we make, becomes the object of our scorn. Some of us say hurtful things so they can hear, others of us under our breath and some only hate in our hearts. But according to Jesus our disdain is no different than murder. How can this occur in the life of a Christian? The strategy is simple, other drivers are stripped of their humanity and they become like the car they are driving—an object, something to be scorned or rejected because of its relative value to us. It follows, if another driver is not really human then why should I apply even the simplest courtesy, never mind considering their holy office in my life? We do not consider that they have lives, and they make mistakes, or even that they have the right to drive slowly if they like. No matter how bad another person drives, they are still loved by God, and our disregard for that fact becomes our own shame. God loves even the worst sinner, and the blood of Jesus is eternal testimony to that.

You may think that I am being extreme, but this is precisely the rationale that human beings have never tired of using as grounds to mistreat others. It has been used to justify the crusades, the holocaust, slavery, and other forms of racism. We are rational people, and the dignity of human beings is evident, God made sure of that. Scripture is clear about that. Therefore, if there is to be systematic denial of basic dignity we have to first dehumanize the target. Humility does not only require the assessment of dignity to all people, but it also requires elevating others to the place of the holy in our life decisions.

There is the misconception that if you do not look out for yourself then no one will. That, however, is not the case. The truth is that if you only look out for yourself no one else will. A.W. Tozer put it this way, "Whoever defends himself will have himself for his defense, and he will have no other. But let him come defenseless before the Lord and he will have for his defender no less than God himself."[137] I might add, what Isaiah said about those who would defend others, "Your righteousness will go before you and the glory of the Lord will be your rear guard."[138] In other words, humility means giving up the right to protect yourself and your own interests. Those you help and your service will protect you from the front, and the Lord himself will cover your back.

chapter 25

the stranger

Religious ethicist, Darrel Fasching, argues that the Bible calls for primary importance to be placed on the stranger. He simply defines the stranger as someone who is different. He emphasizes the biblical ethic of hospitality to the stranger as a sacred responsibility. He proceeds to establish an option that asserts human rights through the irrepressible dignity and holiness of the stranger. In his paradigm, he defines believers as valuing only those on the inside and regarding outsiders as profane. Those who esteem the believer only have no method of integrating people or ideas that are distinct or different. In contrast, this ethic of hospitality to the stranger advocates the active integration of that which is different. The outsider or "stranger" represents the holy and offers the community the only hope for connection God.[139] The image of God is in the stranger, thus, hospitality shown to the stranger (acceptance and attempted understanding) is the welcoming of God into the community. For my community, we have regarded the stranger as the lost and the poor in our lives. Those who are estranged from God and his people or the justice that it implies, are those for whom this rule applies.

By equating esteem of those who are different with intimacy with God, we are offered a biblical solution to the awkward practice of Christian exclusivity. It is the stranger, the non-believer, the poor and those outside the community that is necessary for the community to interact with God. I think this understanding of others is helpful in the pursuit of humility.

The standard way of thinking about humility is to devalue oneself. The resulting attitude is one of inferiority to everyone, and that is humility. As I have argued, humility first requires a divine focus. That alone brings clarity and reveals the truth about ourselves. But how ought we to look at others? Once we realize the truth about our own sinfulness the tendency would be to consider others equally as foul. While this may be true, we are likely to be more understanding of our own shortcomings than we are of others. I am proposing that to be humble one must also consider the best about others.

I have friends who I am very fond of. My best friends make me laugh, and I generally find it easy to appreciate their good qualities. Yet, they too are sinners. Other people I can barely endure. It is almost impossible to ignore their flaws. Certainly my friends can't be more righteous than these other people. No, the more I think about it the more I can admit that my friends often annoy me, but I choose not to reflect on those characteristics. Instead, I remember the things about my friends that I find admirable. However, my good will toward my friends does not actually carry all that much spiritual significance. That's the rub.

In fact, the other group that I find so unpalatable, they are the place of testing for me; they are the mirror from which to assess my own spiritual maturity. So it is not the devaluing of myself that is the key. It is finding a way to value others. One suggestion has been to learn to discover and appreciate admirable qualities in people you know, highlighting in your mind the things about them that are good. However, that exercise can become patronizing and potentially have a negative effect. If in my consideration of you I can only come up with a few noteworthy qualities in your character, the tendency is to consider you inferior to another for whom I can recall several. The result is another judgment that leaves you less than holy.

The solution is a total conceptual revolution of the way we look at others. To see Christ in another is not necessarily to notice the ways that person meritoriously represents Jesus, but rather to simply believe Jesus when he says "whatever you did for one of the least of these brothers of mine, you did for me."[140] It is a total and utter respect that is afforded to every person with whom we come into contact, apparently the weaker the better.

In 1996, my family and I made the decision to move into an economically depressed part of our city. We live where some of our cities neediest live. We have a handful of people from our neighborhood who come over from time to time, which means almost every day we have neighborhood visitors. Usually, it is our joy to welcome them. Sometimes, it is not so easy. There are days when we just don't want to have the responsibility or simply want to be alone. More than anyone, the responsibility usually falls to Monica (my wife) since she is home the most. She never fails to serve whoever comes to our door, not because she is always excited about it, but because of the words of Jesus, which for many years hung over our front door reminding us of the holiness of our neediest visitors, "Whoever welcomes one of these little children in my name welcomes me."[141] Humility means treating others as holy.

Saul Cruz is a remarkable man, and remarkable people are usually accompanied by remarkable stories. When I was in Mexico, I heard several stories about Saul, but this one was particularly remarkable. When Saul was 14, he read John Stott's apologetic, *Basic Christianity*, and he gave his life to Christ. When Saul heard that Dr. Stott was coming to Mexico, he walked a great distance to be able to meet him. He finally arrived at the home of missionaries Doug and Marilyn Stewart who were hosting Dr. Stott and who were also friends of Saul's. It became clear that he could not make it home that evening so the Stewart's suggested he remain there for the night.

The next morning Saul woke to find his shoes had been cleaned and polished. John Stott had tended to his old shoes.

Saul would correspond with Dr. Stott a few times as he grew in his faith and he became a leader in the student movement in Mexico. His leadership role gave Saul the opportunity to attend an international conference in Asia. It was there that he recognized the kind face of John Stott.

Excited, he moved to greet him. Not expecting Dr. Stott to recognize him, he approached with guarded excitement. Once Stott's eyes found Saul it was obvious.

"Saul," he bounded forward to embrace him.

"You remember me?" Saul wondered.

"Of course I do," replied Stott. "I have prayed for you every day since we met."[142]

Perhaps every moment carries with it some pedagogical significance, something that can be gleaned and packaged into an applicable lesson. But there are those rare moments in life when you know that a mystery is being unfolded, and if you do not take notice, you will miss it when Jesus is being revealed by the actions of another, a moment of lucidity, a moment of truth. It must have been that way for Saul that day. Jesus did not live or die for himself, he did it for you and me to the glory of His Father. Jesus reveals a God that irrationally sacrifices his own life for a spiteful creation. Love motivated God to clothe himself in human flesh and to endure mockery and death. Jesus gave his life for us not because he thought our lives were more important than his or that it was economical (one life for many), but because he loved his own. "Although his own did not receive him, yet to them he gave the right to become children of God."[143]

As I have established previously, once God took human form, he redefined what it meant to be human. Therefore everything that he does, in principle as a human, has become the perfect model and the focus of human aspiration. Jesus lived for others. Guided and empowered by his obedience to his Father, God's very heart beat in the chest of Jesus. All that he did was for others.

chapter 26

loved to love

Most of us have known the indescribable joy and liberation that comes from being the object of the affection of God. There is nothing like it. That may be the beginning of our relationship with God, but it is not the end. God, who lacks nothing, does not need our love. His creation remains the apple of his eye, and although they are wayward, he still longs for them to return to him. Therefore, the beloved *of* God are to love *for* God. What we have received freely, we are to freely give. But that is not always how it works.

Too often we become stagnant reservoirs of God's grace, receptacles, where the gift of God is left to spoil. This is not the divine design; it is not the way of Jesus. Jesus loved God by giving himself to others. Sacrifice and service for the sake of another is how Jesus demonstrated his love for his Father. If we would claim to love God, we have to love each other, especially the ones that are unlovable. "This is how we know what love is: Jesus Christ laid down his life for us."[144] If we would claim to love God, we have to elevate the needs of others above our own and see that this is the pinnacle of Godliness, this is humility.

The cutting edge of our faith is found in our interactions with other people, particularly those in need. You can memorize the entire bible or pray and fast for weeks, but you are not putting others before yourself, it is meaningless.

The Bible is so replete with evidence of this truth that it is difficult to decide where to begin. Paul said:

> If I speak in the tongues of men and of angels, but have not love, I am only a resounding gong or a clanging cymbal. If I have the gift of prophecy and can fathom all mysteries and all knowledge, and if I have a faith that can move mountains, but have not love, I am nothing.[145]

Isaiah warned of spiritual exercise that excluded those in need.

> Is not this the kind of fasting I have chosen: to loose the chains of injustice and untie the cords of the yoke, to set the oppressed free and break every yoke? Is it not to share your food with the hungry and to provide the poor wanderer with shelter--when you see the naked, to clothe him, and not to turn away from your own flesh and blood?[146]

Humility is an inward condition that is put to the test when another is in need. If we are like the master, it will not matter where we are going or what we want, the needy will have our attention, our concern and our earnest employment.

Scripture pronounces the least and the last as the presence of God in our lives. How we treat these people becomes the litmus test in which our love for God is determined to be true or false. The other is holy because God himself is party to the interaction.

It was true for Abraham who had three visitors who were the

messengers of Yahweh. For Abraham, their presence was considered an appearing of God himself.

The Lord appeared to Abraham near the great trees of Mamre while he was sitting at the entrance to his tent in the heat of the day. Abraham looked up and saw three men standing nearby. When he saw them, he hurried from the entrance of his tent to meet them and bowed low to the ground. He said, "If I have found favor in your eyes, my lord, do not pass your servant by. Let a little water be brought, and then you may all wash your feet and rest under this tree. Let me get you something to eat, so you can be refreshed and then go on your way--now that you have come to your servant." "Very well," they answered, "do as you say." So Abraham hurried into the tent to Sarah. "Quick," he said, "get three seahs of fine flour and knead it and bake some bread." Then he ran to the herd and selected a choice, tender calf and gave it to a servant, who hurried to prepare it. He then brought some curds and milk and the calf that had been prepared, and set these before them. While they ate, he stood near them under a tree. "Where is your wife Sarah?" they asked him. "There, in the tent," he said. Then the Lord said, "I will surely return to you about this time next year, and Sarah your wife will have a son." Now Sarah was listening at the entrance to the tent, which was behind him.[147]

This promise would be the unlikely fulfillment of the covenant God made with Abraham. The identity of these three visitors is somewhat mysterious. At the very least, they were representatives of God, strangers who were treated as if they were Yahweh himself. This hospitality results in the promise. It is clear from the text that God is directly honored and blessed by the hospitality shown to these men.

Similarly, Lot experienced a divine visitation in the form of strangers.

The two angels arrived at Sodom in the evening, and Lot was sitting in the gateway of the city. When he saw them, he got up to meet them and bowed down with his face to the ground. "My lords," he said, "please turn aside to your servant's house. You can wash your feet and spend the night and then go on your way early in the morning." "No," they answered, "we will spend the night in the square." But he insisted so strongly that they did go with him and entered his house. He prepared a meal for them, baking bread without yeast, and they ate. Before they had gone to bed, all the men from every part of the city of Sodom--both young and old--surrounded the house. They called to Lot, "Where are the men who came to you tonight? Bring them out to us so that we can have sex with them." Lot went outside to meet them and shut the door behind him and said, "No, my friends. Don't do this wicked thing. Look, I have two daughters who have never slept with a man. Let me bring them out to you, and you can do what you like with them. But don't do anything to these men, for they have come under the protection of my roof.[148]

Lot welcomes them, and when the men of the town come to abuse them, Lot is willing to let his own family be wronged before the lives of these men are threatened. The episode does not reveal Lot's contempt for his daughters but rather the association of these strangers with God himself. He would have done anything to care for these visitors because they represented God.

These stories provide the precedent for hospitality to strangers throughout the Bible. Even the writer of Hebrews makes the argument for hospitality based on these narratives. "Do not forget to entertain strangers, for by so doing some people have entertained angels without knowing it."[149]

As usual, Jesus changes things. What was an honor reserved only for those who appeared to be angels becomes the right of all people.

The imposition of entertaining an angel was extremely significant. In Lot's case, it might have even cost him and his family their lives. Jesus requires that all people in need be treated with such care and concern, especially the untouchables. The only time Jesus explained how he, the righteous judge, would come to judge the world, he established this principle. He explained how he would separate the sheep from the goats and the wheat from the tears. What was his means of distinction?—Our treatment of the least.

> All the nations will be gathered before him, and he will separate the people one from another as a shepherd separates the sheep from the goats. He will put the sheep on his right and the goats on his left. "Then the King will say to those on his right, 'Come, you who are blessed by my Father; take your inheritance, the kingdom prepared for you since the creation of the world. For I was hungry and you gave me something to eat, I was thirsty and you gave me something to drink, I was a stranger and you invited me in, I needed clothes and you clothed me, I was sick and you looked after me, I was in prison and you came to visit me.' "Then the righteous will answer him, 'LORD, when did we see you hungry and feed you, or thirsty and give you something to drink? When did we see you a stranger and invite you in or needing clothes and clothe you? When did we see you sick or in prison and go to visit you?' "The King will reply, 'I tell you the truth, whatever you did for one of the least of these brothers of mine, you did for me.'[150]

Jesus is forever associated with the least, by his own choice. Jesus wears his humility with honor. Part of what made him great on earth was his service, especially to the sinners and tax collectors. What makes him great in heaven is the same thing. The cross, which until Jesus bore one, was a symbol of shame and worthlessness. Now it is the symbol of redemption and holiness.

One would think that the blood that Jesus shed would sooner be forgotten. Yet the picture of the triumph of God is different. In Revelation 19 as the final battle is unfolding, heaven is opened and Jesus, accompanied by the army of those he has redeemed, ride on white horses. The redeemed are dressed "in fine linen, white and clean."[151] But Jesus appears, in the fullness of glory and power "dressed in a robe dipped in blood."[152] Jesus wears his humility with honor. Since the cross, Jesus will forever be the Lamb of God. Once a symbol of weakness, it is now our best metaphor for love and dignity. Jesus is not ashamed to love the unlovable, to be seen with them, to share all that he has with them. He commands us to do the same. They are the benefactors of his holiness.

Simply put how we treat the stranger, the outsider, the lost and the poor, those who are different, is how we treat God. This is a vicious truth. The natural conclusion is that we are lost sinners who find that loving the lovely is hard enough, and loving the least is virtually impossible. The good news is that God does not distribute his love based on merit. The foulest of sinners is eligible for the love of God if they will only realize their need. Likewise, we should love without favoritism, not based on merit or personal indebtedness. We are able to do it because we know that we are interacting with Jesus. This, however, is not easy.

chapter 27

self-denial
as ambiton
for others

The Bible is meant to be inspiring. You are supposed to want to achieve things, to let God create through you. There is nothing wrong with ambition. Ambition is good as long as it is not for the advancement of the God we call self. Humility does not mean passivity. Achieve, do great things—for others to the glory of God.

Paul was able to live out this balance. He was certainly a driven man, a man of great ambition. "I have fully proclaimed the gospel of Christ," he wrote in his letter to the Romans declaring, "It has always been my ambition to preach the gospel where Christ was not known."[153] His ambition was for the forgotten, those who had not yet heard. His ambition was for others. I suppose Paul knew the temptation of selfish ambition and warned his churches about it, explaining the necessary contrast between ambition for self and humility. "Do nothing out of selfish ambition or vain conceit, but in humility consider others better than yourselves."[154] His admonition to us has not changed. If humility is to be ours, we must consider others as though they represent the presence of God in our lives.

*A man's pride brings him low,
but a man of lowly spirit gains honor.
-Proverbs 29:23*

chapter 28

strutting
for God

I was a skinny kid. I was about average height, maybe a little short, but not too much meat on my bones. I don't remember when it was that I first learned to strut; it may have been elementary school. I learned quickly that I was either going to be tough, or I was going to be a target. I think a lot of kids have the same experience, especially little boys. We learned that the best way to avoid being beaten up was to appear to be dangerous; you are either predator or prey. Since there was not much of me to be frightened of I learned to use my mouth. Big talk and a certain walk compensated for my small size.

All tough kids have to learn this walk. It is really more of an attitude. It is not something you can learn like ballet or karate. It is more like a state of mind that transfers to the way you walk. As I got older, I would have called it confidence, but it was anything but confidence. Confidence is quiet and unassuming; confidence does not need to be flaunted. We would strut because we were afraid, afraid of looking weak, afraid of our weakness being exposed. You had to learn the walk; it was a defense mechanism, a way of coping. If you have not personally experienced this, just go to your nearest movie theater or mall, where kids hang out. Sit down with a cup of coffee and watch the kids who have learned to strut.

It is not just with kids either. Our culture teaches us all to strut. We are a runway culture. Taught to flaunt what we've got and hide what's missing. The individual is the icon of our country. It never dawned on me to walk with a big friend or to smile at people. It turns out there are other strategies to keep from getting hurt. And maybe getting hurt is not the worst thing that can happen to a person. Maybe strutting has side effects.

Our concept of meekness and humility reveals that we esteem the strong (not the morally strong, the physically, visibly strong). In spite of this truth, walking tall is immeasurably valued. We must at least appear to be invulnerable. This cultural current feeds pride and makes humility extremely difficult to acquire. When I was young I learned to strut to protect myself, but I soon realized it was also a way to intimidate others. When I became a Christian I just began to strut for God. Where I once flaunted my alleged toughness, I now flaunted knowledge of the Bible or feats of spiritual strength.

Jesus would probably have been a strong muscular man. It is likely, that until his inauguration into ministry, at about age 30, Jesus took the trade of Joseph, who was a tekton (day laborer, or construction worker). However, in God's wisdom, before he would begin his messianic ministry, he fasted. Not just any fast but a forty-day fast. This is further evidence that Jesus was ripped. He had to be in order to survive that length of a fast.[156] I have a friend who is a big man, an athlete, who fasted for 40 days. When it was all over, you could barely recognize him, he had lost so much weight. Jesus, who was certainly an imposing physical presence, chose to deprive his body of food and enter his ministry as the picture of weakness and frailty.

I am convinced that he would not have gained much of that weight back. He was now a Rabbi and a traveling one at that. No more muscles. Jesus came in the weakness of the flesh. He shattered every human category for strength. He was not to be like any other leader. He did not strut.

chapter 29

spiritual
pride

It is a brutal irony that confronts us in spiritual pride. Are we so far from the footprints of Jesus that we have forgotten how to walk humbly with our God? Can we really think that it is not a contradiction to prance with our God? Preachers in expensive suits and luxury cars do not conjure up images of the Lamb of God. Bragging Christians do not reflect the savior born in a stable. There is no such thing as strutting for God. The truth is that pride is the pathetic expression of utter ignorance. This is a trustworthy saying: arrogance comes from ignorance.

Paul cautions the Roman church not to consider themselves above the Jews because they are presently responding to the gospel. He warns, "I do not want you to be ignorant of this mystery, brothers, so that you may not be conceited."[157] Paul knew that their ignorance would lead to conceit. Exposed reality finds God exalted and every person desperate. Arrogance is an illusion. It is the worst kind of illusion because it conceals others sins within it. Thomas Aquinas, in his massive work, Summa Theologoia recalls the argument of Isidore.

> Pride is the worst of all vices; whether because it is appropriate to those who are of highest and foremost rank, or because it originates from just and virtuous deeds, so that its guilt is less perceptible. On the other hand, carnal lust is apparent to all, because from the outset it is of a shameful nature: and yet, under God's dispensation, it is less grievous than pride. For he who is in the clutches of pride and feels it not, falls into the lusts of the flesh, that being thus humbled he may rise from his abasement.[158]

In other words, pride is less obvious and more dangerous. We fear it the least, we consider it rarely, and we fancy it more than other sins, when in fact it is itself a fountain of life for all sin and a spiritual disease of epic proportions. This is what John Cassian calls the "mischief of pride,"

> ...Although it comes later in the order of the combat, is yet earlier in origin, and is the beginning of all sins and faults: nor is it (like the other vices) simply fatal to the virtue opposite to it (in this case, humility), but it is also at the same time destructive of all virtues: nor does it only tempt ordinary folk and small people, but chiefly those who already stand on the heights of valor.[159]

Not only is the pursuit of humility stymied by pride but the pursuit of all virtue. We cannot address sin in its various forms without first confronting pride. We must understand that pride is the banner of hell. There will be no one there that can not trace their journey back to pride. It is pride that inspired Adam and Eve to desire to "be like God in knowledge"[160] and by attempting to satisfy that desire, the immortals began to die. Pre-evident to that, pride is the first sin ever committed. Not to mention it is the only sin ever committed in heaven. It was not even an action, just a thought, and it resulted in the expulsion of one third of the host of heaven.

Orthodoxy teaches that Satan is the first to have sinned, and his sin was pride. Unmistakably, pride is satanic. The only remedy for this pervasive and malignant disease is humility. John Cassian makes this point powerfully:

> So God, the Creator and Healer of all, knowing that pride is the cause and fountain head of evils, has been careful to heal opposites with opposites, that those things which were ruined by pride might be restored by humility. For the one says, 'I will ascend into heaven;' the other, 'My soul was brought low even to the ground.' The one says, 'And I will be like the most High;' the other, 'though he was in the form of God, yet he emptied himself and took the form of a servant, and humbled himself and became obedient unto death.' The one says, 'I will exalt my throne above the stars of God;' the other, 'Learn of me, for I am meek and lowly of heart.' The one says, 'I know not the Lord and will not let Israel go;' the other, 'if I say that I know him not, I shall be a liar like unto you: but I know him, and keep his commandments.' The one says, 'my rivers are mine and I made them:' the other: 'I can do nothing of myself, but my Father who abideth in me, he doeth the works.' The one says, 'All the kingdoms of the world and the glory of them are mine, and to whomsoever I will, I give them;' the other, 'Though he were rich yet he became poor, that we through his poverty might be made rich.' The one says, 'I have dried up with the sole of my foot all the rivers shut up in banks;' the other, 'cannot I ask my Father, and he shall presently give me more than twelve legions of angels?'[161]

Forget what you have been told. Jesus' way is better. The way of humility is the way of true strength, and if we would desire to be Christian, the people of Christ, we can not allow pride to live in us. Resist the devil, and he will flee.[162] We must learn to take a posture that honors the memory of Jesus' incarnation and reflects his character to a wondering world. We must be clothed in humility.[163]

chapter **30**

competivness

We live in a culture of competition. Pride is fueled by competition, which is itself fueled by insecurity. This tendency is really the need to be seen as the best or perhaps simply not seen as the worst. C.S. Lewis wrote: "Pride gets no pleasure out of having something, only out of having more of it than the next man. We say people are proud of being rich, or clever, or good looking but they are not. They are proud of being richer, or cleverer, or better looking than others."[164] To one degree or another, we are all involved in this insipid competition.

The concept is so ingrained in the North American ethos that it is almost impossible to speak of competition in negative light. The truth of the matter is that Jesus never promoted competition. Yet, our whole way of life (even the parts we consider Christian) is predicated on this virtue-starving ideal. Our economy, our drive to succeed, and our idea of fun, are all inextricably bound to competition.

I understand that competition produces things. Many of the human race's best technological advances have come because of war, the epitome of competition. Capitalism is based on the idea that when people compete they produce more, and everyone benefits. So, let me get this straight. I am supposed to believe that in order to succeed I have to win, beat the other guy, but that is good for the other guy, which should be my primary motivation—the good of all? Not really cogent is it? If I encourage self-advancement and success in my children at the exploitation and loss of others, how then am I going to appeal to them to live out some grand ethic of human rights?

I am not suggesting an alternative; I am simply pointing out that there are consequences to asserting morality based on competition. It is the same kind of rationale that argues, "I beat my children so they can be stronger and no one in the world will be able to hurt them." That may be true, we do tend to excel under duress, but at what cost do we succeed? What is the price of prosperity, not only to my own sense of morality, but to the lives of others?

The desire to be better than another may result in me getting better grades, or making more money, or driving a better car, or winning a war, but is that the goal? Jesus' life and teaching was directly contrary to the drive to compete. He spoke of compassion and mercy. He taught about giving away and preferring others. Lived out, these ideas are cancerous to competition.

Even in the church, where we tout the ideals of mercy, compassion and humility, pride is fed by the spirit of competition. The problem is so pervasive that the church barely recognizes it. If you do not believe me, then scout some church league softball games, or watch some Christians on the basketball court. I have seen some godly people become vicious (including myself) when a ball and the spirit of competition are introduced. Why is that? Is it because we just do not do well in those settings, or is the setting itself a place of unnecessary testing? Pride, not humility, is fed by competition. Even the popular moralization's of these contests that we teach our children, betray the weakness of the argument. We say, "It's not who wins or loses. It's how you play the game." But if you play well, you will win. We have even created categories to further alienate people between "winners" and "losers." If how I play the game is all that matters then why is being a loser so bad? Don't get me wrong, there is nothing wrong with play. However, if we live out the life of Jesus during these games, we will long to see everyone play well. We will cheer for everyone who is on the court. How would some live out, say, the virtue of mercy on a basketball court?

It is not just in sports either. In some ways, the sports arena only accentuates our lust for success and our drive to win. You can hear it in our conversations. It is called 'one-ups-man-ship.' One person claims to know something or have done something and the other person has to top it. These casual yet endlessly reoccurring conversations often begin with the challenge "I am so busy." So begins the competition to find out just who is the busiest. Or it could be who the rightist is, or the prettiest, or smartest, or most like Jesus. Of course if it's me it's not you. I win, and you lose.

The marketplace can be even more brutal. Friends become rivals; Christians become loveless tycoons all in the name of competition. Years ago there was a cartoon that featured a sheep dog and a wolf. The wolf's job was to eat the sheep and the sheep dog's job was to protect them. When they were both on the job, the sheep dog would always catch and pummel the conniving wolf. But when the whistle sounded, they would clock out and resume a civil and cordial friendship. It is as if Christians want to represent Jesus by doing a job well (which is an excellent goal), but the means to that end are irrelevant. In an effort to win for Jesus, no one has stopped to ask the question: should we? It seems to me that Christians should be different on the job, precisely because they answer to a higher standard and because they refuse to succeed if it means that another will fail. Practically speaking, that means Christians might just get passed up for promotions, who knows? After all, who do we work for? What is our goal?

Jesus never competed with anyone, nor did he advocate it. So it certainly can not guide the Christ follower's life. In fact, what he did instead flips our world upside down. He fancied losing over winning. You could say that he was the consummate loser. He lost power, glory, majesty, freedom, and dignity. Not only that, he preferred losers to winners, picked them as his closest friends and entrusted his ministry to them. (In fact some might say the church didn't start weakening until it got into the hands of some winners.) He brought messages for the sick, the sinner, the blind, the bastard, the prisoner and the prostitute, the leper and the least, the criminal and the collaborator.

He once compared the actions of a woman caught in adultery with the most righteous of a community. He once ignored a man of prominence so that he could thank a prostitute. He dressed like a beggar, lived like a homeless man, made friends with rejects and rejected the friendship of the establishment. He was not handsome, nor rich, not appreciated and he would end his life fittingly, naked and humiliated, stapled to a symbol of disgrace. Yet, this was his revolution (the flipping of our world), a revolution of humility over pride. "He chose the lowly things of this world and the despised things--and the things that are not—to nullify the things that are, (to change) the present order."[165]

Jesus lacked all these things, not because they were out of his reach, but because they were not of real value. He was trying to teach us what we know to be true ourselves; that these things are small—empty. That real value is measured differently.

In Jesus' kingdom we win, but not because someone else loses. We win because Jesus has conquered sin and death and hell. The blood of Jesus was shed and the Holy Spirit was given so that we all could win. Our prize is the life of Jesus, the life that imitates him. The life that cultivates humility and starves pride by refusing to compete the way the world does. Our battle is against sin, in ourselves first, in the world, and in the heavenly realms. Our battle is against pride.

chapter 31

starving pride by acknowledging weakness

All of us have to war against our pride. Our desire to rule over our own lives is at the heart of the problem. Pride has to be disposed as a false king has to be removed from his throne, so that the true King can reign. So pride must be dethroned. It is a long and often difficult process to recognize, but rest assured, God is at work toward that end. The sooner we acknowledge our pride and repent in humility the sooner God will be seated as King, and we can be exalted beside him.

Some years ago, I took a seminary course through an extension of Fuller Seminary in Colorado Springs. Each day there was an informal chapel service, usually conducted by some of the students. It was a summer intensive so many of the seminarians were already working in full time ministry. Some were even pastors who were working on their Doctorate degree. Consequently, we were privileged to hear some pretty good sermons in those little chapel services. My friend, Jon, and

I were the youngest students there, and I can remember acting our age and being particularly goofy one afternoon.

We had just finished a marathon class session that lasted all morning, and the two of us were in full comedic form. Part of what I love about my friend, Jon, is that in one moment we are able to share such rapturous, bladder testing laughter, and in the next, experience the convicting presence of the Holy Spirit. I remember feeling restless and hoping that the chapel would not go too long so we could eat lunch and get outside and exercise. All that changed. In my life, I have probably heard hundreds of sermons, I have seen drama, and I have heard music. But never in my life has one point been so clearly communicated and moved me like what I would hear that day.

One of the Doctoral students got up to speak. He looked to be in his early forties, handsome and articulate. As he began to speak, it was clear that we might be in for a good message. I do not remember his name, but I do remember his story. He began to unravel the last several years of his life before us. He explained how he had been the senior pastor at a large church, which he had built from only a few members. He told us about how God had blessed him and that congregation. He had a wonderful wife and beautiful children, and that he had everything going for him. Until the day he had an affair with a woman in the church. From what he told us, it was one single act of indiscretion. He could not bear the weight of his own guilt and so within a matter of days he confessed to his wife, his staff, the elders and eventually the whole church. He broke all ties with the woman, who left the church, and he asked for help. Not long after that, the church fired him and his wife left him. He tried to reconcile with her, but she was not willing to forgive him. Now, he told us, he was working at trying to pick up the pieces. He was not involved in any ministry but he still wanted to be used by the Lord. So in his spare time, he was coming to seminary and now he was asking God if he could ever find a use for him again.

The story was gripping, but what happened next has written itself forever in my heart and mind. It is the best illustration I have ever heard for this process of deposing pride by acknowledging weakness. He said as a young man he had memorized a poem. He was not sure then why he had memorized such a long and difficult poem but he understood now. He began to recite Henry Wadsworth Longfellow's, "Robert of Sicily."[166] He hung his head and began.

> Robert of Sicily, brother of Pope Urbane
> And Valmond, Emperor of Allemaine,
> Appareled in magnificent attire,
> With retinue of many a knight and squire,
> On St. John's Eve, at vespers proudly sat,
> And heard the priests chant the magnificat.
> And as he listened, o'er and o'er again
> Repeated like a burden or refrain,
> He caught the words, *'Deposuit potentes*
> *De sede, et exaltavit humiles;'*

He became more animated and spoke more quickly.

> And slowly lifting up his kingly head,
> He to a learned clerk beside him said,
> 'What mean these words', the clerk made answer meet,
> 'He has put down the mighty from their seat,
> And exalted them of low degree.'
> Thereat King Robert muttered scornfully,
> ''T is well that such seditious words are sung
> Only by priests in the Latin tongue;
> For unto Priest and people be it known,
> There is no power can push me from my throne!'
> And leaning back he yawned and fell asleep,
> Lulled by the chant monotonous and deep.

The poem had captured us. He went on. The king awakes to find himself alone and locked in the church. Insisting that he is the king and demanding that the door be opened, Robert is instead accosted by the night watchman who believes him to be a drunk. "Haggard, half naked" the despoiled king runs through the streets to the palace, through the gate and into the banquet room. He is enraged to find that another king, physically identical to himself, wearing his crown and royal robes, is seated on his throne. The seminarian gravely recited,

> There on the dais sat another king,
> Wearing his robes, his crown, his signet ring,
> King Robert's self in features, form and height,
> But all transfigured in angelic light!
> It was an angel; and his presence there
> With divine effulgence filled the air,
> An exaltation piercing the disguise,
> Though none the hidden angel did recognize.
>
> A moment speechless, motionless, amazed,
> The throneless monarch on the angel gazed,
> Who met his look of anger and surprise
> With the divine compassion of his eyes;
> Then said 'who art thou? And why com'st thou here?'
> To which King Robert answered with a sneer,
> 'I am the king and come to claim my own
> From an impostor who usurps my throne!'
> And suddenly, at these audacious words,
> Up sprang the angry quests and drew their swords;
> The Angel answered with unruffled brow,
> 'Nay, not the King but the King's Jester, thou
> Henceforth shall wear the bells and scaled cape,
> And for thy counselor shall lead an ape;

Robert would wake to find this was no dream and that he had become a mockery in his own kingdom. For days, Robert lived as the Jester, unrecognized by his own court. His only friend, the ape, assigned to him. Yet, every day he maintained his royal right and demanded that his throne is returned. The angel king would find him from time to time and ask,

> 'Art thou the King?' the passion of his woe
> Burst from him in restless overflow,
> And, lifting his forehead, he would fling
> The haughty answer back, 'I am, I am the King!'

The poem came out of him like a manifesto. What should have after many years been forgotten, seemed to be too woven into his own story for this fallen preacher to forget.

He continued to tell of Robert, how after three years he had remained unwavering about his imperial identity. Accompanying the angel king to the city of Rome, the court encounters Robert's brother, Pope Urbane. Robert rushes through the crowd and confidently points out the impostor to his brother, who to his final shame does not recognize him but instead replies, 'It is strange sport, to keep a madman for thy fool, at court!' The poem closes this way, and this is how we heard it that day. Word for word, passionately intoned:

> In solemn state the holy week went by,
> And Easter Sunday gleamed upon the sky;
> The presence of the Angel, with its light,
> Before the sun rose, made the city bright,
> And with new fervor filled the hearts of men,
> Who felt that Christ indeed had risen again?

> Even the Jester, on his bed of straw,
> With haggard eyes and unwonted splendor saw,

He felt within a power unfelt before,
And, kneeling humbly on his chamber floor,
He heard the rushing garments of the Lord
Sweep through the silent air, ascending heavenward...

And when once more within Palermo's wall,
And, seated on the throne in his great hall,
He heard the Angelus from convent towers,
As if the better world conversed with ours,
He beckoned to King Robert to draw nigher,
And with a gesture bade the rest retire;
And when they were alone the angel said,
"Art thou the King?" Then, bowing down his head,
King Robert crossed both hands upon his breast,
And meekly answered him: "Thou knowest best!
My sins as scarlet are; let me go hence,
And in some cloister's school of penitence,
Across those stones, that pave the way to heaven,
Walk barefoot, till my guilty soul be shriven!"

The Angel smiled and from his radiant face
A holy light illumined all the place,
And through the window, loud and clear,
They heard the monks chant in the chapel near,
Above the stir and tumult of the street:
"He has put down the mighty from their seat,
And exalted them of low degree!"
And through the chant a second melody
Rose like the throbbing of a single string:
"I am an Angel, and thou art the King!"

King Robert, who was standing near the throne,
Lifted his eyes, and lo! He was alone!

But all appareled as in days of old,
With ermined mantle and with cloth of gold;
And when his courtiers came, they found him there
Kneeling upon the floor, absorbed in silent prayer.

By this time, he was crying. So was I. I have heard better recitations of poems. It was not acting that moved us; it was the opposite of acting; it was vulnerability, reality. With transparent courage, this adulterer taught us about humility. His life was no different than mine. He was asking the right question, "Lord can you still use me, a sinner?" It is the first question of humility, the question of deposed pride. The answer of course for the humble is yes. God will exalt those who humble themselves. Circumstances alone are not enough. The king and the pastor could fall from power, but unless they recognized their spiritual poverty, pride remained. The story of King Robert was his story and ours. Spiritual success requires humility. We can not walk in pride and expect to be making strides spiritually. The journey toward Jesus is tread over our pride. Nothing less than its total destruction is prescribed for those who would experience life in the presence of God. It is impossible to be proud and imitate Jesus.

love

My children, I will be with you only a little longer. You will look for me, and just as I told the Jews, so I tell you now: Where I am going, you cannot come. "A new command I give you: Love one another. As I have loved you, so you must love one another. By this all men will know that you are my disciples, if you love one another." Simon Peter asked him, "Lord, where are you going?" Jesus replied, "Where I am going, you cannot follow now, but you will follow later." Peter asked, "Lord, why can't I follow you now? I will lay down my life for you." Then Jesus answered, "Will you really lay down your life for me? I tell you the truth, before the rooster crows, you will disown me three times!

-John 13:33-38

chapter 32

the new command

Love is humility in action. Humility is logically prior to love. It is impossible to love the way Jesus defined love without humility. Love is the natural action of humility, and humility is the result of experienced love. "Nothing humbles the soul as deeply as love."[168]

Within the context of John 13, an incredible and often unnoticed thing happened. Jesus gave a new command. The nature of that new command would change the nature of spiritual life for those who would follow him. Some have argued that since Jesus himself gave up his life we no longer have to, that Jesus gave up everything so that we could have everything here on earth. While it was the will of the Father for Jesus to be humbled unto death, his death meant that we would never have to suffer death. So the argument goes.

The argument is subtly convincing. Yet it is not what the Bible teaches. Jesus did die so that we might have life, eternal life at that.

However, the death he rescued us from was spiritual and eternal. He rescued us from hell. Jesus taught that instead of facing eternal death, if we would die to ourselves, he would be able to live vicariously through us. Jesus' sacrifice also means healing and victory and justice, and even prosperity, but not necessarily now.

The Bible teaches that we are heirs, having the hope of eternal life. That means the riches of God are ours by inheritance, but we have not yet received the fullness of that inheritance. The term implies a future reward, which does produce benefits for the present. The promise brings great comfort and security. It is our hope. However, hope that is seen is no hope at all. Presently we are hard pressed on every side but our hope is in Christ, and it is unseen. For those who are interested in claiming the promises of God, it is important to remember that in this life, Jesus promised that we would have trouble.[169] Pain and suffering are our heritage as followers of Jesus.

I am not saying that miracles do not happen. They do. God still miraculously heals and speaks and even defies nature. He has always done supernatural things, and I see no reason for him to stop now. These things keep us guessing. They make it very clear exactly who God is, and who we are, and that even nature submits to him. But these occurrences are not normative. That is precisely what makes them miracles. We will see moments of supernatural deliverance in our lives with Christ just like he did. But to truly know him means that in every way, we will need to walk the road he walked and drink the cup he drank.

Paul could not separate this truth from knowing Jesus. He purposed to know Christ, which meant to share in his suffering.[170] The life that Jesus lived on earth is to be the life that we lead. Likewise, his eternal life in the presence of the Father is also ours as co-heirs with Christ. It is in the heavenly realms that we are seated with Christ.[171] Please don't misunderstand me. The Christian life is not then a life of sorrow and torment. On the contrary, the life that imitates Christ is the most abundant. It is a life full of joy and peace and the presence of the Holy

Spirit, which Jesus did promise us. This is what makes the life of Christ and the life of a Christian so remarkable. In the face of sacrifice, self-denial, and a life lived for others, the testimony of joy is a moving witness to the New Kingdom of which we are a part. It is a testimony to the power and love of God to sustain and preserve his people in the midst of an evil world.

When the life of Christ is no longer simply referred to but is relived before an arrogant world, the gospel is advanced. The story of the lowly Jesus must be articulated in the language of humility. The truth must be told in love.

chapter **33**

the last
word

In the midst of the drama of the Last Supper, Jesus says the words, "A new command I give you." You would think that these words would have solicited more consideration from those listening, both then and today. "New" means simply, "you haven't heard this one before." This one is special and important precisely because it has not yet been said.

The implications of Jesus giving a new command are mind boggling. It means, first of all, that the 613 commandments of the law are insufficient. It means that Jesus sees fit to add to those commandments, not just interpreting or applying them in a fresh way. Jesus is not explaining an old command—which has been misunderstood--as he did during his Sermon on the Mount.[172] Here Jesus offers an entirely new command. What is even more significant is that Jesus is giving a new command about love. The previous commands that called the devout to love were all encompassing. They were believed to be complete, lacking nothing. Jesus himself said that all the law and the prophets hang on these two commands about love. "Love the Lord your God with all your heart and with all your soul and with all your strength."[173] And the second, which is like it, "Love your neighbor as yourself."[174] The second command is the application of the first. It is what the rich young ruler lacked; it is what John called the evidence of our love for God: our love for others.[175] Jesus was of course right. All of the law could be summed up in these two commands. But there was a new prophet in Israel, and to believe the incarnate God would not leave earth without first radically changing religion as it was known is ridiculous. While those two commands summed up the law and the prophets, those ancient sources were insufficient to reveal this new kind of love, this new command.

What was the new command? "Love one another, as I have loved you." It should be asked, then, "What is new about that?"

For the Greeks and Romans, the command was new because love was not regarded as a chief virtue. The four cardinal virtues were wisdom, courage, justice and moderation. Jesus and the New Testament offered them a distinctly Christian set: faith, hope and love. These became known as the Christian virtues and "the greatest of these is love."[176]

For the Jew this command was new because the old command called for a love of reciprocation (love your neighbor as yourself), but now Jesus is calling them to the highest form of love which is the God-love, the love of sacrifice; "As I have loved you." The love that is being demonstrated as he washed their feet, the full extent of that love, which would be dramatized on the cruel cross, is a love that puts others first.

In the old command, love of self was equal to the love of others. The command required that others receive the same respect and consideration, which a person would afford themselves. This is difficult enough. It meant considering others as equals. Still, today this is the preferred form of love. Even those who are not Christians but have progressive notions about human rights and ethics, ascend to platitudes that assert the equality of all people. Jesus is not content to be the only one who ever understood that self-sacrifice is greater. He told them, "I have set you an example." Love as I have loved you, with utter abandon, without limits, without self-consideration or self-regard. Love recklessly, love to the death.

Love is giving up your own rights, your own life, to another. John was his only disciple that stood with Jesus, accompanied him to Golgotha, and watched as he bled and died.[177] John perhaps better than anyone else understood what love was, because he saw its greatest and most sincere expression that day. John knew that on that day love was redefined, not just for him, or even for Christians, but for the whole human race. "This is how we know what love is...Christ died for us."[178]

Love is humility in action. It is living in the divine hierarchy that means death to the self and life to the soul, in submission to God loving others above ourselves. It is radical and yet plain. There is no other alternative for those who would come after Jesus.

The new command is a call to humility. The substance of the command is love, and its character is humility. The old command called for love too. Love of God and his people. The new command puts self last and includes humility as the defining characteristic for the love we are to show to each other.

chapter 34

the hierarchy
of humility

"Do not think of yourself more highly than you ought," Paul exhorted.[179] He knew that our tendency was not toward accurate self-reflection or healthy introspection, but that we were a people given to exaggeration, especially when it comes to our own perceived merit. How then do we, possessing such obviously biased minds, consider ourselves? The wording of that verse implies that I can, if warranted, think highly of myself. The danger lies in a loss of sobriety.

In that same verse, Paul uses the phrase "sober judgment." Paul does not pretend that all people have the same gifts or that all gifts manifest with the same intensity. No, Paul makes it clear that each person is given a measure of faith and that they should exercise their gift in proportion to that faith.[180] This does not negate or invalidate the significance of each person operating within the context of the body. Each is important. How, then, am I to view myself in terms of a hierarchy of love and service? The answer is: last. The hierarchy revealed by Jesus is God first, others second, and self last.

Self, then, does make the list. As I have said before, self-loathing is not a virtue. Caring for your own needs is necessary. We are the creation of God; you too bear the divine image and are the bride of Christ. To destroy that for which Christ died would be unthinkable, but it is the divine imperative to put the needs and concerns of others before our own. Humility does not demand the destruction of the self, just realignment, to love self last, behind God and others.

Eckart recognized this hierarchy, juxtaposing the inverted values of sinner and saint. "The sinner promotes self by seeking high places of power in a fashionable society, but the sanctified Christian puts God first, others second and self last."[181] We can not continue to consider ourselves in terms of the relative merits of others. Humility instructs us to categorically place our own needs last, behind the needs of others.

I realize that this is not easy or normal. If one were to live this way, it is likely that even the people you serve will find you strange. One might think that such a life of sacrifice and genuine concern for others would be endearing. Perhaps people whom you love and respect will criticize what they see as a pattern of neglecting yourself for the sake of others. My life is far from being the ideal in this matter but many of my life decisions (to puts others first) have been met with scorn and criticism. There are those who will question why you are not looking out more for your own needs, your own advancement, and even chastise you. Although some people are well meaning, some do not care about you, rather they care about the selfish paradigm that you are implicitly challenging. It is not you they are protecting but their own way of life.

Peter once marshaled that very argument against Jesus' announcement that he must suffer and die for others. Jesus' response should teach us once and for all that the way of self-gratification is a hellish version of life. Jesus replied, "Get behind me, Satan for you do not have in mind the things of God."[182] The "things of God" was the redemption of the human race by way of a Roman cross. What friend would have counseled Jesus to bear a cross? If my best friend, who is young and has a promising ministry future before him, told me that he must suffer and die, I would rebuke him too. But what do I know about the ways of God? My rebuke comes from the old paradigm. Paul explained that our attitude (which is the heart of humility) should be that of Christ Jesus, and that we should consider others better than ourselves.[183] In other words, prefer them—let them go first. The relative merit of another is irrelevant; the hierarchy is set. Jesus says that if you love me you will keep my new command.

loving
Jesus

After Jesus gives his new command to love each other the way that he has loved them, Peter says to him, "Lord, where are you going?" Prior to giving the new command he says, "Where I am going you can not come." Peter seems to have ignored the new commandment (which as I have established was quite significant and should have elicited some response from Peter and the others.) Yet, Peter was transfixed on physically, and not figuratively, following Jesus to the place he was going and more importantly learning to imitate him. Jesus allowed Peter to change the subject because he knew where it would lead. Jesus replied, "Where I am going you can not follow me now, but you will follow afterward." Peter objected to this insistence.

Certainly, Peter loved Jesus. He had found himself in Jesus. A stubborn fisherman of little fame, he was hand picked by Jesus and on more than one occasion commended by Jesus and even anointed by

Jesus to lead the other disciples.[184] Jesus had forgiven his presumptions and saw something in him that no one else had. When Jesus was around, I am sure that Peter felt alive, important. He felt like he was somebody. So it was natural for him to resist Jesus' departure. All of Jesus' investment in Peter was coming back to him, and Peter declared his frustration about the possibility of separation and his love for Jesus: "Lord, why can I not follow you now? I will lay down my life for you."[185]

Jesus was teaching about loving others, but Peter wanted to talk about himself and Jesus, just the two of them. It is as if Peter would say, "Yeah, yeah, yeah love others, right okay whatever you say. But, what about you and me, can't we stay together. Can't I just love you some more." Clearly, we don't like loving everyone. We are really more comfortable loving a few people and some of us really only want to love Jesus, because after all, he's the only one who has really always been nice to us. It is obvious that Peter did not love his brothers the way he loved Jesus. Jesus had never wronged him; Jesus was easy to love. In another place, Jesus said "If you love those who love you, what credit is that to you? Even 'sinners' love those who love them."[186] It is our enemies that are difficult to love, those who wrong us, or find us difficult to love.

Peter was willing to lay down his life for *Jesus,* but he ignored the call to love others. Of course, Peter would deny Jesus three times and in the conclusion of John's gospel, Peter is restored as Jesus reminds him of this very conversation. Jesus asked, "Do you love me?" Addressing the one thing of which Peter seemed so sure. "Then love and shepherd and care for my people." Jesus says to all of us who have reason to love him. "If you love me you will obey what I command."[187] And what was the command? Love each other, in humility.

He built the precedent for loving others upon his own merit as the object of our affection. Jesus earned the right to be loved and eternally endeared himself to the human race, first by creating it and then by rescuing it from certain destruction. Jesus knows that we owe him our very lives. Since he lacks nothing, rather than collect on that debt for himself, he calls for that love that is due him to be transferred to others. That is the hard part for us because we are needy. C.S. Lewis calls human love need-love.[188] Love, for us, is inextricably bound to our own need. It becomes a reciprocating love. I need love therefore I give some to you in order to get some from you. Need-love's manifesto is, "I will love you if you love me." God on the other hand, needs nothing. He is sufficient in himself. God does not even need us to receive love, glory, community or even submission. All of these things exist independently within the Godhead. Jesus submits to the will of the Father, the Father glorifies the Son, and the Spirit testifies to them both. The completeness of God must be understood.

This is the context in which we can clearly see the depth of the love of God. God who is the source of all things, and who needs nothing, has chosen to love us. Not because he was lonely or lacked something, but simply because he delights in showing love. It is his divine creative right.

His love then, has nothing to do with need. It is what Lewis calls gift-love.[189] It is one-way love, not reciprocating. This one truth is essential to realizing that God does not, nor can he require repayment for his love. God desires that we would love him because his way of love is better than life.[190] God knows for us to selflessly love means that our life will be better. It is precisely because of the needlessness of God that he calls us to offer his love to others. God is not greedy about love. He is not demanding it all for himself. Quite the contrary, he is casting his own image on the lives of others and saying love me by loving them. The love that is being prescribed is nothing less than gift-love. The love that Jesus showed on the cross and at the Last Supper is the kind of love that constitutes a new command.

The biblical call to love each other is powerful simply in its frequency. If I repeat something, it is because I think it is important and I want you to remember it. Scripture inundates the reader with its tireless theme of love.

Just by looking at the verses that use words "one another" reveals the quality and character of this love that we are called to...

Be devoted to one another in brotherly love. Honor one another above yourselves. Romans 12:10

Live in harmony with one another. Do not be proud, but be willing to associate with people of low position. Do not be conceited. Romans 12:16

Therefore let us stop passing judgment on one another. Instead, make up your mind not to put any stumbling block or obstacle in your brother's way. Romans 14:13

Accept one another, then, just as Christ accepted you, in order to bring praise to God. Romans 15:7

You, my brothers, were called to be free. But do not use your freedom to indulge the sinful nature; rather, serve one another in love. Galatians 5:13

Be completely humble and gentle; be patient, bearing with one another in love. Ephesians 4:2

Be kind and compassionate to one another, forgiving each other, just as in Christ God forgave you. Ephesians 4:32

Submit to one another out of reverence for Christ. Ephesians 5:21

Bear with each other and forgive whatever grievances you may have against one another. Forgive as the Lord forgave you. Colossians 3:13

Therefore encourage one another and build each other up, just as in fact you are doing. 1 Thessalonians 5:11

And let us consider how we may spur one another on toward love and good deeds.
Hebrews 10:24

Now that you have purified yourselves by obeying the truth so that you have sincere love for your brothers, love one another deeply, from the heart. 1 Peter 1:22

This is the message you heard from the beginning: We should love one another. I John 3:11

No one has ever seen God; but if we love one another, God lives in us and his love is made complete in us. I John 4:12

Words like devotion, honor, harmony, submission, acceptance, agreement, forgiveness, service, kindness, compassion, gentleness, patience, admonition and encouragement are all expressions of this inexpressible virtue we call love.

This life changing call to love without repayment, to love in spite of our own need, can be vexing. The only way that we can love like God is if all of our needs are first met by him and our satisfaction is in him. We have to first realize that he is our source, that he is himself our provision, our portion of love, and not others. Our joy must safely reside in the love of the Father. This was the secret of the man, Jesus, who daily received life and love from the Father and remains today the living portrait of true and selfless love. He was the master of love born from humility. When God is both the source of the love we receive and the love we give, then God is exalted, and we are humbled. Humility is both a product and predecessor to love. It is a product because as we love we recognize our utter dependence on God. It is predecessor because we can not love others without first humbly receiving the love of God. We are only able to love because he first loved us.[191] John Wesley concluded,

Nothing humbles the soul so deeply as love: It casts out all 'high conceits, engendering pride;' all arrogance and overweening; makes us little, and poor, and base, and vile in our own eyes. It abases us both before God and man; makes us willing to be the least of all, and the servants of all, and teaches us to say, 'A mote in the sun-beam is little, but I am infinitely less in the presence of God.'[192]

notes

Chapter 1: The elusive truth

[1] Andrew Murray, Humility, p. 37

[2] C.S. Lewis, Mere Christianity, p.109.

[3] Exodus 10:3, Proverbs 6:3, Daniel 10:12, James 4:10.

[4] 1 Corinthians 4:7.

[5] C.S. Lewis, Mere Christianity, p.109.

Chapter 2: The divine paradigm

[6] The Antichrist.

[7] Ibid.

Chapter 3: Moving toward humility

[8] James Stewart, Life and Teaching of Jesus Christ, p. 204.

[9] Lewis, Mere Christianity, p.114.

Chapter 4: Imitation

[10] Charles Spurgeon, Sermons, no. 2328.

[11] G.K. Chesterton, Heretics, p.90.

Chapter 5: The inner life

[12] Matthew 23:5-12.

Chapter 6: Inside the cup

[13] John 12:24.

[14] 1 Samuel 16:7.

[15] Galatians 2.

[16] Tertullian, The Ante-Nicene Fathers, Vol.3 p.1244.

[17] Spurgeon, Sermons, no. 2328.

[18] John Calvin, Institutes of the Christian Religion, p. 846.

Chapter 7: Humility begins with Awe

[19] Rudolf Otto, The Idea of the Holy, p.12.

[20] Romans 1:19-20.

[21] Lewis, The Problem of Pain, p. 20.

[22] Romans 1:21.

Chapter 8: Theophany

[23] Job 26:6-14.

[24] James 3:13.

[25] Isaiah 6:1.

[26] Isaiah 6:5.

[27] Job 42:5-6.

[28] Luke 5:8.

[29] Matthew 28:9.

[30] Revelation 1:17.

[31] Ezekiel 1:28.

[32] Isaiah 6:7.

[33] Isaiah 6:9.

[34] Job 42:12.
[35] Luke 5:10, Matthew 16:18.
[36] Matthew 28:19.
[37] Revelation 1:17-19.
[38] Ezekiel 2:1.
[39] James 3:14-15.
[40] John 8:44.

Chapter 9: The Divine Center
[41] Spurgeon, Sermons, no. 2328.
[42] 2 Corinthians 4:6.
[43] Calvin, UI, p. 852.

Chapter 10: Neonizing God
[44] 1 Corinthians 3:16.

Chapter 11: The incarnational life of worship
[45] Ephesians 5:1.
[46] John 1:14.
[47] John 14:9.
[48] Ephesians 5:2.
[49] Ephesians 5:2.

Chapter 12: A life transformed by the gospel
[50] Kim Lawton, "Faith Without Borders," Christianity Today, May 19, 1997.
[51] Johnstone, Operation World
[52] Lawton.
[53] Ibid.
[54] 2 Corinthians 5:17.

Chapter 13: A life that imitates Jesus
[55] Nahum 1:5.

Chapter 14: Given completely to God

[56] Tim Dowley, Ed., Erdman's Hand
[57] John Piper, Let the Nations Be Glad. book to the History of Christianity, p. 442-444.
[58] Luke 9:24.
[59] Tom Sine, Live It Up.
[60] John 13:15.
[61] Psalms 95:6.
[62] 1 Peter 5:5.

Chapter 15: The self-revelation of God

[65] Ibid.
[63] Brad Goldstein, The Saint Petersburg Times, May 16, 1998, p. 1B.
[64] Ibid.
[66] Romans 8:37.
[67] Dallas Willard, The Divine Conspiracy.
[68] Donald Kraybill, The Upside-Down Kingdom, Herald Press, 1978.

Chapter 16: The humility of God

[69] John 5:19.
[70] John 5:30.
[71] John 6:38.
[72] John 7:16.
[73] John 7:28.
[74] John 8:28.
[75] John 8:42.
[76] John 8:50.
[77] John 14:10.
[78] John 14:24.
[79] Colossians 1:15.
[80] Philippians 2:9.
[81] Stewart, Life and Teaching of Jesus Christ, p. 207.
[82] The Nicene Creed.

[83] Passages like Mark 1:34, 43, 3:17, 5:43, 7:36, 8:30, 9:9 et al., commonly referred to as "the messianic secret."
[84] Jonathan Edwards, Sermons.
[85] Galatians 2:20.
[86] John 14:10.
[87] John 1:1-2.
[88] Stewart, p. 78.
[89] John 1:18.
[90] 1 John 1:1.
[91] Lewis, Mere Christianity.
[92] Ibid.
[93] Stewart, p. 209.
[94] Thomas A. Kempis, The Imitation of Christ, p. 90.
[95] 1 Corinthians 2:1-5.

Chapter 17: Denying yourself

[96] Calvin, Institutes, p. 1390.
[97] Jonathan Potter and Margaret Wetherell, Discourse and Social Psychology, p.14.

Chapter 18: Deifying the self

[98] Genesis 18:27.
[99] Job 19:20.
[100] 2 Corinthians 12:11.
[101] John 5:30.
[102] Kempis, p.90.
[103] Psalms 42:3.
[104] John Wesley, The Complete Works of John Wesley, Vol. 7, p.168-9.
[105] Romans 12:2.
[106] Matthew 16:24, Mark 8:34, Luke 9:23.

Chapter 19: Living a contradiction

[107] John 16:33.

[108] John 13:17.
[109] Revelation 2:10.
[110] James 4:8-10.
[111] Kempis, p. 90.
[112] Romans 8:13.
[113] 1 Peter 3:18.

Chapter 20: Embracing the truth
[114] Hebrews 12:2.
[115] Romans 12:3.
[116] Colossians 1:24.
[117] 2 Timothy 2:11-12.
[118] Chesterton, Orthodoxy "Suicide of Thought".

Chapter 21: Believable truth
[119] Matthew 10:33
[120] James Patterson and Peter Kim, The Day America Told the Truth, p. 144.
[121] Ibid.
[122] 2 Peter 2:13-15.
[123] 1 Timothy 5:18.
[124] Galatians 4:12, 2 Thessalonians 3:9.

Chapter 22: The power of self-denial
[125] J.B. Lightfoot (translation), The Martyrdom of Polycarp.
[126] John Cassian, The Works of John Cassian.
[127] Taylor Branch, Pilar of Fire, p. 255.
[128] e. g. King's final speech.
[129] C.T. Vivian, (Personal Communication).
[130] Sharon Kay Dobins, "The Principles of Equality and the Sermon on the Mount as Influence in Ghandi's Truth Force," The Journal of Law and Religion, 6, p.131.
[131] Martin Luther King Jr., "Strength to Love", p. 53.

[132] Luke 22:42.
[133] Romans 12:17, 21.
[134] Lightfoot, Polycarp.

Chapter 23: The holy other
[135] Genesis 18:2.

Chapter 24: His image
[136] Ephesians 2:14.
[137] A.W. Tozer, The Pursuit of God, p.28.

Chapter 25: Stranger
[138] Isaiah 52:12.
[139] Darrel J. Fasching, The Coming of the Millennium, (Valley Forge, Pennsylvania: Trinity Press International, 1996), p. 35.
[140] Matthew 25:40.
[141] Mark 9.37.
[142] Personal Communication.
[143] John 1:12.

Chapter 26: Loved to love
[144] 1 John 3:16.
[145] 1 Corinthians 13:1-2.
[146] Isaiah 58:6-7.
[147] Genesis 18:1-10.
[148] Genesis 19:1-8.
[149] Heb 13:2.
[150] Matthew 25:32-45.
[151] Revelation 19:14.
[152] Revelation 19:13.

Chapter 27: Self-denial for others
[153] Romans 15:20.

[154] Philippians 2:3.

Chapter 27: Self-denial as ambition for others
[154] Philippians 2:3.

Chapter 28: Strutting for God
[155] Proverbs 29:23.
[156] Personal Communication

Chapter 29: Spiritual pride
[157] Romans 11:25
[158] Thomas Aquinas, Summa Theologoia, P(2b)-Q(162)-A(6)-RO(3)
[159] Cassian, The Works of John Cassian.
[160] Genesis 3:5.
[161] Cassian, The Works of John Cassian.
[162] James 4:7.
[163] 1 Peter 1:5.

Chapter 30: Competitiveness
[164] Lewis, Mere Christianity, p. 109-110.
[165] 1 Corinthians 1:28.

Chapter 31: Starving pride by acknowledging weakness
[166] Henry Wadsworth Longfellow, "Robert of Sicily," all excerpts taken from, Favorite Poems of Henry Wadsworth Longfellow, p. 119-125.

Chapter 32: The new command
[167] John 13:33-38.
[168] Wesley, The Complete Works, p.64.
[169] John 16:33.
[170] Philippians 3:10.
[171] Ephesians 2:6.

Chapter 33: The last word

[172] Matthew 5:21-43.
[173] Deuteronomy 6:5.
[174] Leviticus 19:18, Matthew 22:39.
[175] 1 John 4:20.
[176] 1 Corinthians 13:13.
[177] John 19:25-26.
[178] 1 John 3:16.

Chapter 34: The hierarchy of humility

[179] Romans 12:3.
[180] Romans 12:6-8.
[181] Eckart, A Presentation of Perfection, p. 16.
[182] Mark 8:33.
[183] Philippians 2:3.

Chapter 35: Loving Jesus

[184] Matthew 16:18.
[185] John 13:37.
[186] Luke 6:32.
[187] John 14:15.
[188] Lewis, The Four Loves.
[189] Ibid.
[190] Psalms 63:3.
[191] 1 John 4:19.
[192] Wesley, The Complete Works, p.64.

LaVergne, TN USA
06 February 2011
215464LV00004B/1/P